FANTASTIC UNIVERSE

JANUARY 1959
Vol. 11, No. 1
Hans Stefan Santesson
Editorial Director

SAUCERIAN PUBLISHER
Original Sources in Ufology

ISBN: 978-1-955087-37-7

9 781955 087377

2022, Saucerian Publisher

Fantastic Universe was a U.S. science fiction magazine published in the 1950s. It ran for 69 issues, from June 1953 to March 1960, under two different publishers. It was part of the explosion of science fiction magazine publishing in the 1950s in the United States and was moderately successful, outlasting almost all of its competitors. The main editors were Leo Margulies (1954–1956) and Hans Stefan Santesson (1956–1960); under Santesson's tenure, the quality declined somewhat, and the magazine became known for printing much UFO-related material. A collection of stories from the magazine, edited by Santesson, appeared in 1960 from Prentice-Hall, titled The Fantastic Universe Omnibus.

Fantastic Universe published its first issue in the midst of this publishing boom. The issue, published in digest format, was dated June–July 1953, and was priced at 50 cents. This was higher than any of its competition, but it also had the highest page count in the field at the time, with 196 pages. The initial editorial team was Leo Margulies as publisher, and Sam Merwin as editor; this was a combination familiar to science fiction fans from their years together at Thrilling Wonder Stories, which Merwin edited from 1945 to 1951. The publisher,King-Size Publications, also produced The Saint Detective Magazine, which was popular, so Fantastic Universe enjoyed good distribution from the start—a key factor in a magazine's success. The first issue included stories by Arthur C. Clarke, Philip K. Dick, and Ray Bradbury. According to Donald Tuck, the author of an early SF encyclopedia, the magazine kept a fairly high quality through Merwin's departure after a year and through the subsequent brief period of caretaker editorship by Beatrice Jones. Margulies took over the editor's post with the May 1954 issue.

In October 1955, Hans Stefan Santesson, an American writer, editor, and reviewer, began contributing "Universe in Books", the regular book review column. A year later, with the September 1956 issue, Santesson took over from Margulies as editor. One immediate change was an increase in the number of articles about UFOs. Santesson ran several articles by Ivan T. Sanderson, including articles on auras and the abominable snowman. However, he also ran polemical writings opposed to the UFO mania, including strongly worded pieces by Lester del Rey and C.M. Kornbluth. Del Rey, at least, felt that Santesson was not a believer in UFOs: "So far as I could determine, Santessen was skeptical about such things, but felt that all sides deserved a hearing and also that the controversies were good for circulation."

The quality of the fiction is thought by Donald Tuck to have generally fallen during Santesson's period at the helm, though this was not entirely his fault—a great many other magazines were competing for stories by the top writers. Santesson himself, despite a modicum of controversy over his heavy use of UFO and related material, was kind and helpful to writers and was well-liked as a result.

In late 1959 the magazine was sold to *Great American Publications*, and it was significantly redesigned. The size was increased to that of a glossy magazine, although the magazine was still bound rather than saddle-stapled. Under King-Size Publications, the magazine had had no artwork except small "filler" illustrations; now interior illustrations complementing the stories were introduced, and photographs and diagrams accompanied some of the articles. A fan column by Belle C. Dietz, began, and Sam Moskowitz wrote two detailed historical articles about protosf. However, the March 1960 issue was the last one Fredric Brown's "The Mind Thing" had begun serialization in that issue; it was eventually published in book form later that year.

Circulation figures for *Fantastic Universe* are unknown since at that time circulation figures were not required to be published annually, as they were later. After the magazine folded, the publisher entertained plans to publish material bought for the magazine as a one-shot issue titled "Summer SF"; however, the issue never appeared. Santesson later edited an anthology from the magazine, titled *The Fantastic Universe Omnibus*.

Great, but unpretentious, this title is an extraordinarily rare symbol of what was going on in those early years of the modern UFO phenomena.

Editor
Saucerian Publisher, 2022

INDEX

INTERNATIONAL ASTRONAUTICAL FEDERATION

WE WOULD normally bring you the story behind the cover on this page, but this month Harry Harrison, noted science fiction editor and writer, tells you that story in his THE ROBOTS STRIKE and we, instead, report to you on the thinking of some of the men for whom Tomorrow is a reality!

Scientists, engineers and lawyers representing twenty nations, including the United States, Great Britain and the U.S.S.R., have just taken part in the ninth congress of the International Astronautical Federation which met in Amsterdam, in the Netherlands, from August 25th through the 30th, 1958.

While topics discussed ranged from rocket and satellite technology to anticipated space-law problems, there was much informal debate, in the corridors and in the meeting rooms, on ways and means by which European and other countries could join in space research. A NATO-sponsored programme was one obvious possibility, as was the possibility of cooperation between the British Commonwealth countries.

A warm reception was given to Dr. Wernher von Braun, who was making his first appearance at an I. A. F. Congress, and who spoke on the Explorer Satellite project, outlining the general characteristics of the Jupiter-C four-stage carrier.

Professor L. I. Sedov of the U.S.S.R., discussing the "Dynamic Effects of the Motion of Earth Satellites," dismissed as small the effect of the sun and the moon on artificial satellites. In determining the Sputniks' orbit, he reported, 60,000 measurements had been processed from radio measurements and about 400 from optical observations for Sputnik 1; 12,800 radio measurements and 2,000 optical observations for Sputnik 2; and, as of July 7, 1958—52,750 radio measurements and 1,260 optical observations for Sputnik 3. These data were processed on high-speed electronic machines and the elements of the orbits computed.

Participants in the Congress included Dr. James Van Allen of Iowa State University, Professor S. F. Singer of Maryland University, A. R. Hibbs of the Jet Propulsion Laboratory of the California Institute of Technology, R. E. Roberson of North American Aviation's Autonetics Division, Professor Fred L. Whipple, and others. Professor Singer raised the possibility that cosmic rays may be responsible for the radiation belt which is considerably thinner at higher latitudes and absent at the poles. This meant, he said, that if launchings were made from the polar regions rockets could escape up a virtually radiation-free "tunnel." He warned, however, that if subsequent experiments confirmed his theories, the operation of manned satellites would not be feasible between altitudes of 250 and 40,000 miles without heavy biological shielding, which would render any such project entirely impracticable. The possibility of "sweeping out" the radiation, by sending up large satellites which would absorb any protons encountered, was also discussed.

SPECIAL OPPORTUNITY for NEW subscribers

ENJOY MORE
S. F. and FANTASY
by MORE
GREAT WRITERS
in this
MONEY SAVING OFFER

8 ISSUES
FOR ONLY $2.
PLUS
AN EXTRA ISSUE
FREE
IF YOU REMIT NOW
AS BELOW

Here's an EXCITING invitation to bring into your home the world's greatest SCIENCE FICTION MAGAZINE! You can now have FANTASTIC UNIVERSE delivered to you at a special low price that saves you almost one-third of the price you would pay on the newsstand!

As a FANTASTIC UNIVERSE reader you get the most thrilling stories by such masters as Isaac Asimov, Judith Merril, Theodore Sturgeon, L. Sprague De Camp, John Brunner, Lester del Rey, Harry Harrison and many others of the greats.

* * * * *

FOR—the greatest possible variety each month within the range of SCIENCE FICTION and FANTASY by both your old favorites and our new discoveries....

FOR — interesting discussions with your friends of the exciting new stories in every breath taking issue, while they too are still under the enchanting spell of its prophetic magic....

FOR — the absolute delight of the fabulous cover designs of many world-renowned Science-Fiction artists together with their own 'Story about the Cover.'...

TAKE ADVANTAGE of this money-saving opportunity by mailing the coupon right NOW. This exceptional offer assures you of receiving at low cost, the finest Science Fiction and Fantasy of the kind you will not want to miss.

MAIL THIS COUPON TODAY

KING-SIZE PUBLICATIONS, Inc.   91
320 Fifth Avenue, New York 1, New York

Yes! I want to receive FANTASTIC UNIVERSE at your special money-saving rates! Please enter my subscription checked below.

___ 8 issues of Fantastic Universe for just $2. Please bill me.

___ Enclosed is $2. Send me 9 issues of Fantastic Universe. (A saving of 36% of the regular newsstand price.)

Name_____

Address_____

City_____ Zone____ State_____

FANTASTIC
UNIVERSE

JANUARY 1959
Vol. 11, No. 1

H. L. Herbert
Publisher

Hans Stefan
Santesson
Editorial Director

Virgil Finlay
Cover Design

FANTASTIC UNIVERSE, Vol 11, No. 1. Published bi-monthly by KING-SIZE PUBLICATIONS,
INC., 320 Fifth Ave., N. Y. 1, N. Y. Subscription 12 issues $3.75, single copies 35¢. Foreign
postage extra. Reentered as second-class matter at the post office, New York, N. Y. The
characters in this magazine are entirely fictitious and have no relation to any persons living
or dead. Copyright, 1958, by KING-SIZE PUBLICATIONS, INC. All rights reserved. Jan., 1959.

PRINTED IN U. S. A.

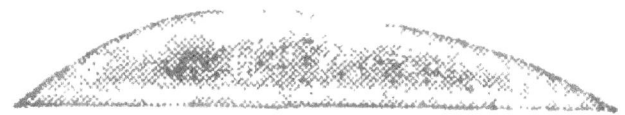

trade

mission

by . . . Daniel F. Galouye

They would be ready to sit down and discuss quietly their mutual problems only after this display of might.

CHURNING the virgin atmosphere of Atlas-III, the two formidable fleets roared down from the ebony depths of space.

The glittering duralloy ships of Merope-IV contracted into a cluster of shimmering motes. Supported by flagellate strands of fire, they backed down on roaring jets. They landed on the northern edge of a dismal plain, hemmed in by desolate peaks and ridges.

More furtive in their descent, the dark-colored vessels of the Electra-VI fleet drifted down languidly in an anti-G approach. They hovered briefly over the southern edge of the rugged expanse, then slipped softly to the surface, scarcely stirring the dust of the bleak plain.

A bay slid open in the nose of the Meropean flagship. Ominous needles of fierce light lanced out. And three mountain peaks to the east erupted in cataclysmic nuclear explosions.

The Electran flagship went into action. A vivid purple beam pierced the naked atmosphere. It swung slowly, intently along a mountainous ridge. And, in its wake, the jagged outcroppings became ignescent. The molten rock formed

---

A number of writers have suggested that we will bring with us, Tomorrow, many of the attitudes, magnified, which seem to be characteristic of these days. Be that as it may, Dan Galouye returns here with this story of a rather unusual trade conference, set in a far distance future.

---

serpentiform rivulets that writhed down the craggy slopes.

Another Meropean ship sent three dread Z-missiles streaking into the upper atmosphere. Their glowing surfaces left faint zig-zag lines of light that stood out like clear pencil marks against the blue-black sky. Auto-controlled, the projectiles disappeared and reappeared as they slipped ephemerally into and out of hyperspace in intricate random evasive patterns.

Three more lances lunged from the same ship, vanishing into hyper scarcely a hundred yards above the plain. Their re-emergence into normal space was barely detectable, since they reappeared in each instance but a microsecond before they slammed into the elusive Z-missile targets.

The resultant blasts, like tiny novas, were still visible against the velvet shroud of space when the Electran flagship, in another contemptuous gesture, suddenly generated a fiercely coruscating force shield. It spread bubblelike to encompass the entire fleet.

It was the beginning of a Merope-Electra trade conference.

And if the other sixty-four civilized worlds of the Pleiades Cluster had known the parley was taking place, they would have been tensely awaiting its outcome. But every stage of its planning had been cloaked in secrecy.

The conference site was on a barren plain of Atlas' uninhabited third world.

There it would be decided, across the conference table of course, which of the two contending powers would emerge as commercial kingpin of the cluster.

But only when the display of might was over—only after military potentialities had been thoroughly demonstrated — would the trade commissions of the two worlds be ready to sit down and submit their differences to enlightened and sensible negotiations.

THE Meropean Ambassador Eriksen had the floor. He was a tall, severe man whose rigid bearing and jutting chin belied the weakness and complacency implied by his soft, gray hair.

His face was sharp, his eyes quite blue and intense, and his complexion inordinately pale. Clearly evident in his features were the inherited characteristics of the Earthly Nordic stock that had emigrated across long light years of space, under sponsorship of the Norswefin Trading Corporation, to colonize Merope-IV.

"In pursuance of the peaceful aims embodied in the Meropean Charter," he was saying soberly, "I hereby present my credentials as the duly authorized principal delegate to the Merope-IV—Electra-VI trade conference, convened here this Galactic Day of—"

Across the table, Ambassador Schar-El rose, pulling on his chiseled beard.

"We don't need all that fancy

talk, Eriksen," he said crudely. "We know what we're here for. Let's talk plain. The recorders can sew lace on the words later on."

The Electran envoy indicated the two clerical assistants, one attached to each delegation and seated between the respective ambassadors and military attaches.

Schar-El was dark-skinned and blank-faced. His features were wrapped in an inscrutably rigid expression which, like those of all Electrans, scarcely altered no matter how imperative the emotional stimulus.

He wore a fiery red robe with purple border and a bejeweled turban that served more to house communication equipment than for ornamental purposes.

"Very well," Eriksen agreed, setting aside the official scroll. "We'll do it up frankly. Anyway, we'll be more likely to get our meanings across that way."

He glanced at Admiral Leighart and received a sanctioning nod from the military attache.

Outside, the barren plain stretched away equidistant on both sides of the conference hut to the opposing fleets. Over all hung a tenuous mist —the residue of exhaustive weapons demonstrations.

And Ambassador Eriksen viewed the haze with no small degree of satisfaction. The Electran weapons had been formidable. But most of them were not new. And, in all, he had seen nothing to challenge Meropean military superiority—un-

less the robed ones were holding back.

"You list your demands," Schar-El said abruptly. "Then we'll list ours. That's the general procedure, I believe."

Eriksen unbuttoned his coat and started by rote. "Number One: Merope demands all trading privileges and unlimited concessive rights to the interstellar commerce now originating on the two inhabited planets of the Alcyone system. Electra-VI to withhold, if so disposed, local interplanetary and satellitic rights and privileges.

"Number Two: All trading privileges and unlimited concessive rights to Maia-III. Secondary rights to be available to Electra . . ."

After he had gone through all sixty-four civilized worlds which had, until now, been under the commercial hegemony of either Merope *or* Electra, he added:

"Further terms of the proposed compact require that Electran interests withdraw all permanent trade commissions from all the aforementioned worlds."

Eriksen glanced at Admiral Leighart, who smiled back with smug approval.

The Electrans had not moved a facial muscle. Sometimes their complete lack of overt emotional response, the Meropean ambassador conceded, could be quite disconcerting.

Schar-El rose. "Gentlemen, our counterproposals — Number One: All trading privileges and unlimited concessive rights, et cetera, et cetera and so forth, on Alcyone-II and -III. Merope to hold local interplanetary and satellitic rights. Number Two: Same arrangement for Maia-III . . ."

Item for item, the demands paralleled those listed by Eriksen until the spiel ended with, ". . . Merope to withdraw all permanent trade commissions from the aforementioned worlds."

AMBASSADOR Eriksen didn't like it at all. The scowl on his face indicated as much. The Electrans had never exuded so much confidence before. It could only be that they *were* holding back some superweapon.

And the fact that they hadn't demonstrated it might indicate the Electrans considered it so formidable that they *actually desired* an immediate armed showdown—an intracluster war.

Were they ready for war, Eriksen wondered, as much as Merope was? Or more so?

Admiral Leighart tugged at his sleeve. "Ask them if they intend to show off any more stuff."

"Can't," the envoy whispered back. "Weapons are never discussed at these conferences. They are there to see, but never are they mentioned diplomatically."

Schar-El rose again. "Well, what's with it, Erik? Do we haggle now—or later?"

"I think that since we know each other's position," Eriksen said stiffly, "we should retire for consultation with our commission staffs."

The Electran ambassador touched his turban politely. "As you wish. But I think there is at least one thing we may agree on now. That's the matter of mutual assurance that the security of this conference hasn't been compromised by Earth agents."

"Earth," Eriksen assured, "has learned nothing about the details of this meeting from any Meropean source. You have my word for it."

"I can guarantee the same," Schar-El returned. "And that is just as well. Of course, you realize that keeping Earth out of this is to our mutual benefit. This way, we'll settle our differences in private."

Eriksen smiled and thought grimly: To the victor goes the spoils, without any stray jackals around to hog in on the feast.

Then his reflections assumed a more serious tinge: Sanctimonious, meddling, smug Earth, with the awful power of the Solarian fleet behind her, would force arbitration of the Meropean-Electran trade differences if she knew a critical conference was taking place.

Moreover, Earth was in a position to prevent war by bringing economic pressure to bear against both worlds. Terra would do that to protect its own interests throughout the Pleiades. But damned if they could pull any strings after the whole cluster was ablaze with interstellar war!

The Meropean ambassador wondered, however, why *Electra* had been so stupidly agreeable to a private settlement. As weak as they were, comparatively, he should think they'd be more than willing to welcome the supervisory influence of Earth over the dispute . . . unless, of course, Schar-El *really had* something in the form of a superior weapon tucked neatly away under his secretive turban.

The whole setup smelled. And it troubled Eriksen no end.

IN the wardroom of their flagship, the principals of the Meropean delegation paced odd, isolated circles, each pausing occasionally to stare out the port at the dismal, barren landscape. It was late afternoon and already Atlas was riding low on the bleak horizon, shrouded in the gathering nighttime fog.

"I don't like it at all," Eriksen said forlornly. "They're too confident, too cocky."

Secretarial Recorder Jensson spread his hands helplessly. "How can you tell? They never show anything on their faces."

Admiral Leighart clasped his wrist behind his back. "We should have held some of our big stuff in reserve. We didn't have to bare practically all our teeth in one big splurge."

"You think they're holding back something?" Eriksen cupped his chin pensively.

Leighart shrugged. "I'm not quite sure," he said unsteadily.

To Eriksen, there was something slightly pathetic about seeing the tall, lean Meropean military commander displaying uncertainty. It didn't fit in well with his stern features, his meticulously pressed uniform, his gleaming black boots, all the lustrous medals.

ACROSS the plain, a fierce light sprang up suddenly and all three men crowded the porthole. The surging brilliance that had shattered the gathering dusk was a full-phase force shield. It was taking rapid shape around the only battered ship the Electrans had brought along with the fleet—an outdated, decrepit tanker.

The shield, however, wasn't antiquated. It was the best the enemy could generate. But it was inadequate—pitifully inadequate—against the meson beams that played against it from two other Electran vessels.

Suddenly the vivid, pulsating shell collapsed and the tanker disintegrated—a falling heap of dust.

"Neat, neat," mumbled Eriksen, impressed.

"Can we do better than that?" the recorder asked, worried.

Eriksen answered with confidence. "Our shields are much stronger than theirs. They could hold up against ten times as much firepower."

Admiral Leighart, however, shook his head somberly. "But we don't have any guns that can pierce one of their full-phase shields," he reminded.

The ambassador fumed. "Then show them something else! And it had better be good enough to offset what we just saw!"

Leighart mumbled something about getting near the bottom of the barrel, then shouted orders into the intership mike. And the three delegates crowded the port again to watch the adjacent Meropean ship.

It shimmered momentarily, then slipped into total invisibility—all except the forwardmost ten feet of its bow. Eriksen glanced over at the normal- and hyper-radar screens. There was no blip representing the ship on the latter. On the former, only the ten-foot section remained where, moments before, the entire vessel had been visible.

"Radar can't track it?" he asked hopefully.

The admiral shook his head and smiled proudly. "It's totally, completely protected from detection. To all practical purposes, it simply doesn't exist—not here in normal space, not out there in hyperspace. One section was allowed to remain visible, of course, to convince the enemy the ship *is* still there."

"Ingenious!" Jensson complimented. "That ought to make them take notice."

Eriksen rubbed his hands together enthusiastically. "I'm sure, gentlemen, that tomorrow we'll see a more conciliatory attitude on the part of the Electrans."

The admiral grinned. "You think we'll be able to have our total war after all?"

"Of course."

"You're sure Merope won't be satisfied with concessions?" Leighart asked worrisomely.

The ambassador patted him on the shoulder. "You'll have your sport, Admiral. Don't worry about that. We'll settle for nothing less than the opportunity to loose our fleet against them. We don't want simple concessions—not even total concessions. That would give them the chance to perfect better weapons. All we want the conference table to produce is an excuse to go to war."

But Leighart's face sagged. "I wonder," he said pensively, "whether Schar-El isn't at this very moment telling Admiral Devon-Ama that the Electrans don't want concessions—that *they*, too, want only an excuse to declare war."

The recorder, however, lightly laughed off Leighart's ominous dejection. "I think we've got them good this time."

Eriksen smiled profusely. "We'll stick by our demands. We won't budge an inch. We'll watch them back down to the point where they'll have to fight for economic survival."

But there emerged from the mist outside the ship at precisely that moment something which made the ambassador choke back all the confidence he had felt surging up within him.

It was a mammoth automaton, vaguely human in form and proportions, but towering above the tallest Meropean vessel!

THE fiery coat-of-arms of Electra-VI was emblazoned arrogantly on its breastplate. Girding its waist like a spiked band was a battery of mesotronic beam generators.

The square surface of its shoulders served as twin mounts for Z - missile launching muzzles. Twelve-foot-long pedal plates were equipped with pulverizing spurs and spikes. The arms were crude battering rams and their appearance left no doubt that their intended purpose was to destroy brutally.

And, surrounding its massive bulk, was an almost imperceptible aura—evidence of a new-type force shield the likes of which Eriksen had never seen before.

The thing stood brazenly in front of the flagship, its cold, lifeless eyes seeming to stare curiously in through the porthole.

"Good God!" Leighart gasped.

"That must be it!" Recorder Jensson exclaimed. "That must be what they were holding back!"

Bravely, Eriksen struck a pose of partial composure. "Come now, gentlemen. You've seen a robot before."

"But, God!" Jensson protested apprehensively. "Not like *that!*"

"Look!" Leighart extended a trembling finger toward the ship's detection screen. "It's out there—completely visible—but it doesn't show up on the scope!"

Outside, Eriksen and the admiral respectfully kept their distance from the metal colossus as they strained their necks to stare up at its frozen features.

"No wonder Schar-El could afford to play it cagy at the conference table," the admiral offered dismally. "I could too, if I had something like that."

Eriksen gestured hopefully. "It could be a bluff. It might be just a giant piece of animate machinery with dummy weapons. It . . ."

His voice trailed off despairingly as he realized the futility of his wishful thinking.

"How do you suppose they got it here?" Leighart backed off fearfully.

"In pieces. Aboard several ships. That's why they came in on an anti-G approach. Couldn't do any reaction maneuvering with that kind of a load."

Leighart stiffened abruptly. "You think it's here to smash our fleet?"

"Of course not. That would violate the protocol of these conferences." The ambassador was acutely worried, though. It was evident in the fathomless lines in his forehead, in his disheveled hair, rumpled from running his hands distraughtly through it.

"Sending the thing past the midway point between the fleets violated protocol," the admiral reminded tartly.

And that it did, Eriksen realized wryly.

The automaton hadn't shifted a limb. But now its head—almost obscure in the swirling evening mist—was inclined and 'it seemed to be staring condescendingly at the general and the ambassador.

"Should we protest to the Electrans—about this intrusion?" Leighart asked.

Eriksen made a snorting sound. "And degrade ourselves? Let them know we're perturbed? Of course not. Anyway, if we ignored protocol and asked about a military weapon at a trade conference, it would convey the impression we are completely unnerved."

They were silent a moment.

Then the ambassador turned to Leighart. "Since Schar-El has provided us with the opportunity, let's test the thing. Order the flagship to concentrate a double mesotronic barrage against its shield. Ye'll see what happens."

The admiral relayed the order through his portable comgear as he and the ambassador backed around the flagship.

Twin beams lashed out from the nose of the vessel, splaying viciously against the automaton's breastplate. But the incredibly thin shield held stubbornly.

"Very well, then," Eriksen swore. "They asked for it. We'll get rid of that thing in short order —without any more playing around. Admiral, have the flagship relay range data to every gunner in the fleet. I want all mesotronic generators turned full against that hunk of metal!"

He drew Leighart further around to the rear of the vessel.

The dull mist of the plain came alive in writhing fluorescence as the full shield-busting strength of the fleet exploded mercilessly against the target.

When Eriksen and Leighart returned around the flagship, however, the automaton still stood there— unperturbed, its faint force shield continuing to glow almost imperceptibly, as though nothing had happened.

"Well," said the ambassador dispiritedly, "I think we'd perhaps better make a concession or two tomorrow."

"What!" Leighart protested. "You mean there might not be a war after all?"

"I mean nothing of the sort. We'll merely try another tack. By making concessions, we can observe their behavior. The nature and extent of their reactions may give us a clue as to just how formidable that thing is."

Abruptly, the ground around them convulsed and rumbled as violent gushers of pure white flame spouted from the automaton's ankles and pedal plates.

The massive hulk recoiled slowly from the ground. The flames roared out more forcibly. And the walking arsenal lunged lancelike into the murky sky, its acceleration at least matching that of the best Meropean dreadnaughts.

"Good God!" Admiral Leighart shouted. "Not only is it an attack mechanism and a mobile bastion. It's a ship too!"

Later that night, as Eriksen and Leighart and Jensson paced odd, isolated circles in the wardroom of their flagship, they heard the hollow booming and harsh *zip-zip* of the Electran guns sounding out across the plain.

"Listen to them celebrate!" the ambassador said morosely.

ERIKSEN'S face was barren, almost as expressionless as Schar-El's and the other two Electrans' who sat across the table from him.

"Upon reconsideration of our position," the Meropean envoy was saying, "we have decided it would be in the best interest of our government if we amended our proposals somewhat."

He glanced up and thought he saw the merest beginning of a smile forming on Schar-El's implacable face. But he couldn't be certain.

"Therefore," he continued, "we wish to cancel our demands for all trading privileges and unlimited concessive rights to the Maia, Alcyone and Taygeta systems. We are willing to accept local interplanetary and satellitic rights and privileges, if Electra is so disposed to grant such rights therein."

He cleared his throat solemnly. "However, we insist on preeminent rights on the other sixty-one worlds of the Pleiades Cluster and will make no further modification of our proposition."

For a moment Schar-El's impassive face wrestled with incipient emotion. If the expression were allowed birth, Eriksen knew, it would be one of malicious satisfaction.

The Meropean ambassador turned to gather his delegation. The conference was over for the day. The Electrans would need time to weigh the altered proposals.

But there was a rustling of brocaded material as Schar-El brushed his robe aside and gained his feet.

"We are quite willing to bend a bit too," said the Electran envoy. "You may strike out our demands for all primary rights in the Randour, Zargan and Listel systems. We'll manage with the secondary stuff in that area."

His voice lowered somewhat. "But we still insist that all permanent Meropean trade commissions be pulled off the other sixty-one planets."

Confounded, Eriksen watched the Electrans march out and head across the plain for their fleet.

Admiral Leighart gripped the envoy's arm. "What do you make of it?"

"I think," Eriksen said pensively, "they are a good deal more cunning than we imagined."

"But why are *they* making concessions?"

"Either they're toying with us— savoring victory," Jensson suggested, "or there's some flaw in their automaton and they want to end the conference in a hurry before it shows up."

Eriksen snapped his fingers. "That's it! They're trying to get as much as they can out of us, then rush a compact through the mill before we catch on!"

"But if there is a flaw," the admiral said disconsolately, "we'll never find out what it is. They've shown their trump card. They won't expose it again!"

But the recorder disagreed. "I think they will. I rather imagine they'll risk exposure to coerce us into a quick signature so they can get the hell out of here with their loot."

Eriksen smiled. "I believe you're right, Recorder. Shall we return to our quarters and prepare for a revisitation by that tin monstrosity?"

JENSSON'S prediction wasn't wrong.

The automaton returned at precisely the same time it had appeared on the previous evening. Eriksen and Leighart had been waiting on the bridge of the flagship. The Meropean fleet had been rearrayed along the circumference of an imaginary circle, all its attack weapons trained radially inward.

The surface redeployment had been executed in full view of the Electran fleet before the nocturnal mist had closed in. The maneuver was intended as a challenge. It had embodied the threat: "We are prepared. Now let's see you send your impregnable weapon into the circle of destruction."

The implied challenge had obviously not been ignored. The automaton came.

Still not registering on the detection screens, it materialized, apparently from hyper, scarcely a hundred yards above the surface and descend-ed in an anti-G approach. The ground shook and imparted the vibrations to the hulls of the Meropean vessels as it thumped down on the rocky plain and strode to the exact center of the circle.

But the Meropeans were prepared.

"Now!" whispered Ambassador Eriksen.

"Now!" shouted the admiral into the intership gunnery control circuit.

It was havoc such as had never been brought to bear on a single target before—multiple mesotronic beams, devastating and fiercely brilliant cosmo-K shafts, hellishly zigzagging lances from the subelectronic rifles, the blindingly silent blasts of a thousand photon generators, the insufferable roar of the projectile launchers.

And when it was all over, when the radiant aftereffects and sparking discharges had finally played themselves out, when the smoke and mist and dust had settled, the automaton remained — impeccably undisturbed.

Its shining metallic armor was unscarred, not even scorched. And the Electran insigne on its breastplate was even more derisively visible than before.

Distraughtly, Eriksen turned toward the admiral, who was sourfaced and subdued. "It's impossible, Leighart! *Nothing* can stand up under that kind—"

Suddenly the admiral was stark naked before the envoy. And they weren't on the bridge of the flagship any longer.

Eriksen was successively aware of the painful pressure of his bare feet against sharp rocks, of the darkness of the night, the looming shadows of the Meropean vessels all around them, the confounded swearing of the hundreds of officers and thousands of men from those ships—all nude and helpless and afraid in the cold night.

"My God!" Leighart groaned, looking around for the automaton that was no longer there. "It's got hypnotic control too!"

Eriksen numbly listened to the jubilant roaring of the Electran guns as they cut loose with barrage after barrage in confident celebration of their assured diplomatic victory.

"I THINK," said Eriksen meekly at the conference table the next morning, "that Merope is prepared to make additional concessions."

Schar-El sat up sharply and spread his hands tensely on the table. His face may have been an immutable mask, but his blanched knuckles betrayed his expectancy.

Beside him, Admiral Devon-Ama and Recorder Celeb-Karn were equally anticipative.

Stripped of all diplomatic propriety by his lack of composure, the Meropean ambassador went on:

"We'll get out of the following systems—El-Attara, Silverdot, Cartright, Sandstone, Shangri-La, Utopiastar, Wamby, Moorehouse . . ."

He paused to catch his breath.

And Schar-El, apparently thinking he had finished his list, rose. "Very well, Ambassador. We'll drop our claim on Bittersby, Remote, Angara, El-Brightsun, Crossroad, Hellenback, Sarona and Inbetween."

He filled his lungs and brusquely added, "but that's as far as we'll go, mind you. No farther."

BACK in the Meropean flagship, Eriksen paced and repeatedly banged his fist into his palm.

"What are they trying to do?" he demanded of no one in particular. "What is their strategy? Why the concessions?"

Jensson spread his hands. "They came to this conference with certain minimum requirements. They know what they want. This is their devilish way of getting it."

"When they could have *everything?*"

The recorder glanced uneasily down at the floor.

"Maybe," he proposed hesitatingly, "we had them figured out wrong. They might be—fair, just. They may be willing to share the cluster and not freeze us out completely."

"Or," Admiral Leighart interposed more pointedly, "maybe—as formidable as their automaton is— maybe it *does* have an Achilles' heel."

"Like what?" Eriksen asked skeptically.

"Like—why, like—well, maybe—" Leighart shrugged.

"Well," Jensson offered, "perhaps we'll have another chance to find out."

But the ambassador tensed distastefully at the thought of another encounter with the thing.

BY the time evening came, though, Eriksen had drowned most of his apprehension in determination and anxiety. He wanted the thing to come back — eagerly, desperately.

In preparation, he had dispatched four teams of technicians, all equipped with personalized anti-G packs and special tools into the misty night air to await the automaton's arrival.

And, obligingly, it made its third visitation. More obligingly — as though it knew the ambassador's intentions and was quite willing to accommodate them—it had its force shield turned off.

Eriksen pressed hard against the thick glass of the porthole and watched the juggernaut come down. Then he stiffened incredulously as the flagship's spotlight centered on the robot, illuminating its features in sharp detail.

"Leighart!" He grasped the admiral's arm. "Look! On its breastplate!"

The admiral filled his lungs with a startled, rasping breath. "The Meropean insigne!"

Eriksen's eyes narrowed in humiliation and he clenched his fists bitterly. "It's their contemptuous way of saying, 'Don't you wish it was yours?'"

Admiral Leighart swore. "Only a twisted Electran mind could dream up that kind of insidious insolence!"

The ambassador's stare was riveted so scornfully on the mocking coat-of-arms that he scarcely noticed the teams of technicians drifting up alongside the towering metal form.

Three Meropeans alighted on the right shoulder. Two on the left. Five came down on the skullplate. Two more settled on the ridge formed by the band around its slim waist. One tried to force his way beneath a kneecap and thereby gain entry into the vulnerable interior.

Hopefully, Eriksen began to imagine that the crews might succeed—might work their way into the electronic guts of the thing and disable it.

With a thorough knowledge of how its various offensive and defensive features operated, they could conceivably discover its Achilles' heel. Or, they might learn enough about it to duplicate the thing and thereby compromise the enemy's advantage.

But suddenly the great right forearm elevated and swung around in a swatting motion. Metal palm clanked against metal breastplate. And, when it withdrew, there was the crushed form of a Meropean technician splattered against the plate.

Horrified, Eriksen watched it swat again and again, as though it were plagued by a swarm of insects. When it had rid itself completely of the pests, it disdainfully brushed off its armor and dusted its hands. Then it turned away nonchalantly and disappeared into the mist with long, leisurely strides.

Ambassador Eriksen sank brokenly into a chair and let his arms flop limply between his legs. His jaw hung uselessly open and he stared unseeingly across the compartment.

"They're not sticking by the rules," Leighart observed hoarsely.

Eriksen shook his head numbly. "No. They're not."

"But—but that means they might attack—right here—now—any minute!"

"They—they might at that," the ambassador admitted insensately.

"Then let's get out of here! Let's run!"

"Won't do any good. We wouldn't stand a chance. I don't think Merope stands a chance."

"But what are we going to do?"

"Pray that they let us live through the night so we can crawl back to the conference hut tomorrow."

ERIKSEN stood trembling imperceptibly before the huge, polished table. His usually neat hair was unkempt, his face haggard. His shoulders lumped and his head was bowed.

Beside him, Admiral Leighart was similarly depressed as he sat with his hands resting flaccidly on the table, his back arched and his head inclined in a most unmilitary manner.

Jensson successfully hid his feelings behind a flurry of action with the recording keyboard.

"All right," the Meropean ambassador said submissively, "what do you want?"

Schar-El, across the long table, folded his arms and stared into his lap. "We were hoping we could gain rights to—a few of the worlds."

Eriksen heard Leighart swear softly and whisper, "Damn them! They're going to stretch it out—make us give up the cluster system by system so they can enjoy every single concession!"

The Meropean envoy silenced him with a wave of his hand and turned back to the Electrans.

"Very well, then," he went on futilely. "In addition to the concessions we made yesterday, we are prepared to relinquish all claims on the systems of Melpomene, Erato, Augusta, Euterpe, Eisenhower, Polymnia, Eiffel, Thalia . . ."

Naming the worlds one by one was a humiliating drudgery. And it was made all the more mortifying by the stony stares of the faces across the table. He could only wonder at the intensity of jubilant emotions that the Electrans must be concealing at this moment.

He reached the half-way mark in his list of the sixty-four worlds and paused to stare beseechingly at the opposing delegation.

And he thought sadly of Merope and its plans for economic empire and how all was beyond recovery now. And he wondered how he would ever explain it to the Emperor.

Eriksen's eyes moistened and he turned back to the roster of lost worlds.

"You're going to concede more?" Schar-El asked suddenly.

And the Meropean envoy could only guess at the stark sarcasm and intense gloating behind the question.

"You know very well that we are," he replied dully.

"But we are satisfied. We are satisfied." For a moment there seemed to be a tinge of urgency in the Electran envoy's words.

"You mean," Eriksen asked incredulously, "you don't want *all* the worlds?"

Schar-El only stared silently back at him.

"Test their sincerity!" Eriksen heard Admiral Devon-Ama whisper anxiously. "Test it!"

The Electran recorder worked furiously on his instrument and finally produced two official-looking sheets of printed paper.

Admiral Leighart leaned closer to Eriksen. "They've prepared a final draft! They're ready to sign!"

"But we've only conceded half the worlds!"

Recorder Jensson spread his hands. "It's like I told you. They *don't want* to crush us. They're fair. They're satisfied with a just share of commerce."

Eriksen fell back into his chair. It was inconceivable. Yet, from all indications, Jensson was right.

Ambassador Schar-El hurried around the table, his brilliant robe swishing around his silver-trimmed boots. He thrust the document into Eriksen's hand.

The Meropean envoy studied the twin sheets of paper. It *was* a fair division of trade rights! The compact split the cluster equitably between Merope and Electra.

Eagerly, he signed both copies, unable to convince himself that this wasn't only an illusion—that some unguessable treachery wasn't brewing.

Schar-El signed the documents and, with a ceremonial flourish, handed one over. "We knew, Ambassador, that Merope would be fair about this."

It was, Eriksen realized, a final expression of stinging sarcasm, meant to chasten the Meropean delegation for having come to Atlas-III seeking war.

Schar-El signaled to Admiral Devon-Ama and Recorder Celeb-Karn and the trio hurried from the conference shack.

It was fully a minute before anyone in the Meropean delegation stirred.

"Well I'll be damned!" said Leighart.

"We've a lot to be thankful for," proposed Jensson.

Eriksen shook his head unbelievingly. "We certainly have. But now we face an even more difficult job ahead of us."

The other two stared questioningly at him.

"Telling the Emperor about the

position we're in with super-automations in the Electran arsenal," the envoy explained, "and convincing him how fortunate we are that the Electrans are fair and peaceloving."

AMBASSADOR Schar-El paced the bridge of the Electran flagship, hardly conscious of the grid-streaked void of hyperspace that was slipping by beyond the observation ports.

"I can't believe it!" he muttered incredulously.

Admiral Devon-Ama glanced up from the chart. "It can only be that they *are* reasonable and honorable after all."

"But — but that's impossible! They've always been warmongers. Up until this trade conference we knew they were out to pick a fight!"

"Then we were wrong, that's all. Our intelligence slipped up."

Schar-El, scarcely hearing the admiral, continued pacing. "And then, when they get the one superweapon that gives them unchallenged supremacy, they do an about face and agree to share everything fifty-fifty."

Devon-Ama plotted a sphere of position on the chart. "Forget it. We were simply lucky. Let's just be thankful that they didn't want war after all. With a fleet of automatons like that, they could have wiped out every trace of Electran culture in the entire cluster."

"None of our guns could dent it! Nothing we had could disturb it!"

"Nothing *they* had could disturb

it either. They showed us how invulnerable it was by first cutting loose at it with all their firepower every time they decided to send it over for a demonstration."

Schar-El shook his head disconsolately. "If only we could have captured it!"

"We tried."

"Maybe we didn't try hard enough."

"I'm sure we did. As it is, you're going to have trouble justifying the loss of thirty-two men."

ON the Meropean flagship, Recorder Jensson slipped stealthily aft. He paused in the corridor, checked to see that he wasn't being followed, then darted into the gear compartment set against the outer hull.

He produced a minuscule instrument from his jacket and held it against the bulkhead.

"Fox calling Big Stuff," he whispered into the tiny grid.

"Big Stuff," the instrument rasped back at him. "Go ahead."

"Success. Everything worked out as anticipated."

"Fireworks?"

"There won't be any. Jumbo performed too well."

"Splendid. Where is the thing now?"

"Sector Five Remote was controlling. I guess they've dispatched it back to Earth by now."

"So they did—I just got the report. It's due back here tomorrow."

The voice paused a moment.

"Incidentally, that was good work."

"Thanks, but I didn't do anything. I just went along for the ride."

"You made a vital contribution toward staving off a major war in the Pleiades for at least a generation. You gave us a correct estimate of the situation when Jumbo's insignia-changing control got stuck."

"All I did was guess how the Meropeans would react when they saw their own insigne on a weapon that was—uh, killing Meropean technicians. I felt sure they'd simply regard it as a mocking gesture."

"You guessed right. And, as a result, we were able to continue with our original strategy."

"What about the thirty-two Electrans and twenty-eight Meropeans the others were hypnotized into believing were killed?"

"They're all en route to Earth in Jumbo's passenger compartment. They'll be psychically reoriented and assimilated into systems outside the cluster."

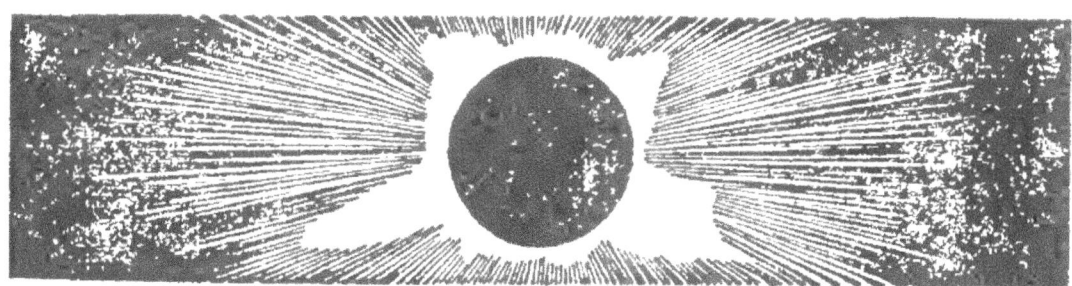

OUR LITTERBUG SUN

ROCKET ASTRONOMY is discovering evidence that our sun is a litterbug. That the sun is ejecting hydrogen gas in vast flares, hydrogen gas which ends up in what has been called Earth's "front yard" and right in the way of all the planets of the solar system. In other words, space is not quite so empty as we've believed.

Dr. Herbert Friedman and his associates at the United States Naval Research Laboratory in Washington have developed a new, a third kind of astronomy, based on observations made with rockets rather than with ground telescopes or with the recording of radio waves from space. The rockets are equipped to "see" only ultraviolet light of a kind considerably more powerful than the one that gives you that lovely sunburn.

A hundred miles or further up in space, the ultraviolet "eyes" see space become aglow with intense light, the glow an ultraviolet light of a wave length which does not reach the earth because it is filtered out by the air. The rocket eyes measure the intensity of this light. When the rocket's instruments are turned to a higher wave length, they can "see" through the glow, locating distant stars and galaxies "as blobs of radiation."

ward

of

the

argonaut

by ... L. Sprague de Camp
and Fletcher Pratt

He was looking for the girl he loved. That was all. What may have been unusual was the manner of his looking.

MR. COHAN set a boilermaker down in front of Mr. Gross, who was holding Professor Thott, Mr. Witherwax, and Mr. Keating from the library, if not exactly spellbound, at least immobile.

". . . so the next day," he said, "a flock of trucks drove up and unloaded those statues on my Uncle Max's lawn. So my Uncle Max is stuck with ten cast-iron statues of an ugly guy named Hercules, wearing a second-hand tiger, all because he couldn't leave well enough alone. So when I heard about it I said to myself, Adolphus Gross, let that be a lesson to you to leave well enough alone, and I done it ever since."

He paused for effect, sipped the rye and took a gulp of the beer.

Witherwax said: "The trouble is if everybody did that we wouldn't get anywhere."

"I only meant—" began Gross. Witherwax was not to be stopped.

"For instance," he said, "I was reading in a book how somebody invented distilling. If they left well enough alone we'd be drinking wine or beer and there wouldn't be any gin, and Mr. Cohan couldn't mix me another dry Martini. Oh, Mr. Cohan!"

L. Sprague de Camp and the late Fletcher Pratt collaborated on a series of stories published, some years ago, as TALES FROM GAVAGAN'S BAR. *Here is a hitherto unpublished story from Gavagan's—where the impossible is the only predictable possible, where anything can happen—and usually does.*

The voice of the bartender, who was farther down, talking to a customer, became louder, as though he were indicating to Witherwax that the cause of the delay was inescapable: "No, I'm telling you I have not seen her tonight, nor last night, nor the night before that. And if ye want to talk to the rubber plant, it's your own right, because everything is free in Gavagan's saving and excepting the liquor. Jim, get Mr. Holland that step now."

He came down the bar toward Witherwax, but like the three other habitués of Gavagan's, that gentleman was watching in fascination as the bar-boy produced a small kitchen step-ladder on which the neatly-dressed young man climbed to place his head on a level with the small rubber tree that grew in a pot on a bracket just above the window-curtain.

"Althea!" he said distinctly, "I'm here." He gazed at the rubber tree.

"Who is he?" asked Witherwax.

"It's a Martini you're wanting?" said Mr. Cohan. "Him? Oh, that's Mr. Holland, and all that money of his doing him no more good than if it was made of mud."

"Is he crackers?" asked Gross.

The young man had climbed down again and apparently caught this remark, for he shook his head with a melancholy smile. Witherwax said: "Ask him to have a drink with us. Nobody should be that sad in Gavagan's."

Before Mr. Cohan could proffer the invitation, Professor Thott stepped over to the young man. "Sir," he said, "I offer the proper apologies for the apparent rudeness of one of my companions, and request that any injury be dissolved in a libation."

The young man hesitated, considered, said: "I suppose I might as well," and followed Thott to where the others were waiting. Introductions were made; he would have a double stinger. It was not until he had taken the first sip from it that he turned toward the circle of expectant faces.

"I don't blame you for thinking I'm bats," he said. "I don't even mind. Perhaps I am. But she was real. You've seen me with her, haven't you, Mr. Cohan?"

"That I have," said Mr. Cohan. "And as decent a girl as I ever put eyes on. You would be sitting all the time at the corner table there, and minding your own business that had the world and all to do with each other."

Holland swallowed the rest of his double stinger at a gulp and pushed his glass back for a refill. Witherwax cleared his throat. "If you could tell us . . ." he said.

I don't know that it will be much help, to me or to you (said Holland), but I'll try. I'm looking for the girl I'm in love with, and I'm afraid I'll never find her because I think she's a—dryad.

(*He let the last word drop separately and searched the faces of Thott, Witherwax, Gross and Keat-*

ing, as though to see whether any-one was being scornful or skeptical. No one was. Holland drank from his replenished glass and began again.)

I'll tell you and see what you think. I have a little money, you know. It's handled by one of those investment trusts, which shifts some of it from one holding to another once in a while. I believe that money should be as responsible as any other part of our economy, so instead of just sitting around drawing dividends or going in for racing cars and chorus girls, I've made a hobby of checking up on the firms my money is invested in, taking an active part as a stockholder, and informing myself well enough so that I can ask intelligent questions of management at meetings.

A little while back the trust informed me that they had put me rather heavily into the Acme Real Estate firm—not a controlling interest, but a strong minority—and so, as usual, I went around to see how they operated. I found they were a management corporation, specializing in office buildings, so I continued my checking by going around to the buildings to see how well they were run.

One of them was the Ogonz Building, over on Lattimer Street; fifteen-story job. When I went over it, there were two things that struck me particularly—seemed to give the place a personality of its own, which most office buildings lack. One was the immense flagpole on the roof,

surmounted by a big golden eagle. You can't see it at all from most of the adjacent streets because ·you can't get enough—what's that word sculptors use when they stand back from their statues to see how they're coming?

(*"Recul," said Thott; "or is it receuil? Speaking of things French, Mr. Cohan, I think I will vary my procedure by having a jorum of Hennessey."*)

I got there about seven o'clock after having run over several other buildings, and the second thing that made an impression on me was the night elevator man. He looked like a cross between a gnome and a land-mine, a solid figure with heavy hips, rather spindly shanks, knock knees and a great mass of curly black hair over a dark face. He was quite suspicious; wouldn't let me in at all until he'd checked by phone with the night man at Acme.

I didn't think that was too bad a characteristic in a man with his job because places have been burglarized in just that way, so I let him see it was all right with me as he took me around. Of course, when we reached the roof and saw the flagpole, I exclaimed about it. His face went even darker than before and he muttered something.

"What's the matter?" I asked. "Don't you like it?"

He talked with a rather thick accent, but I gathered that he did like it, very much. What he was angry about was that orders had been given to cut the pole down. His rage over it seemed somewhat out of proportion, but as soon as he told me, I got mad, too. All the way down in the elevator, I kept getting madder at the thought of destroying that splendid pole with the golden eagle.

By the time he let me out, I was really simmering. I told him not to worry; that pole was going to stay there even if I had to throw somebody out of a job to keep it there. I meant it, too, and the next morning I went around to Acme and told the girl in the outer office that I wanted to see Sherwin, the president, about the flagpole on the Ogonz Building.

He's one of these big lemon-blonde businessmen, very pompous, who sits back from his desk, just caressing the edge of it with his belly.

"You are interested in acquiring the pole?" he said. "We are taking it down, but it is a relic of some historical value."

I said: "No, I'm just here to ask you not to take it down. I like it there. By the way, if you look at your books, you'll find I'm a major stockholder in your company."

He puffed a couple of times and said: "Well, Mr. Holland, it's not very usual for stockholders to interfere with the minor details of management. I think you may trust our discretion in protecting your financial interests. As a matter of fact, both the direct cost of continually replacing the flag on that pole and the labor cost of having a man raise and lower it each day are appreciable items, on which we propose to effect a saving."

By this time I was really annoyed. I told him that my interest was not financial but personal, and if he effected any savings that way, I was going to buy up enough more Acme stock to have control, and he could go do his saving for somebody else. He huffed and puffed around so much over that, that in order to calm him down, I asked him what it was a relic of.

He was smooth. "I've addressed the Advertising Club on that topic at one of our little five-minute informal speeches," he said. "The flagpole on the Ogonz building is a single stick of cedar from the island of Samos in Greece. It was originally a mast on the Greek sailing training ship *Keuranos,* which was visiting this country when Greece was invaded, and after the war was found too unseaworthy to make the return voyage. Mr. Pappanicolou, the restaurant man, was then owner of the Ogonz Building, and he secured the mast as a flagpole. I believe there is more to the story, which I do not seem to remember at the moment, but the night man at the Ogonz Building can inform you. He was one of the sailors on the *Keuranos.*"

I thanked him for that much and went away. Mr. Cohan, will you provide for me once more?

(*Keating said into the interval: "Samos, eh? That's where they had the famous temple to Hera, isn't it? The one in the grove, where the priestesses were called dryads?")*

Whether they were or not (continued Holland, sipping). Yes, I've looked it up myself since. Anyway, the pole stayed up, and it's still there, and all I've had to do is turn down Sherwin's attempts to get me to lunch with him at the Advertising Club about once a week.

The next event in the series was that I went to a cocktail party at the Mahers and met Althea, Althea Dubois. I suppose most men think the girl they fall in love with is the most beautiful object on earth, but Althea really is. Slender and not very tall, with one of those triangular faces and rather light brunette hair. The moment I touched her hand I knew this was it, and the next moment she was looking at me hard out of a pair of green eyes and saying: "Aren't you the Mr. Holland who stopped them from taking down the flagpole on the Ogonz Building?"

"Why, yes," I said. "Are you interested in it, too?"

"Very much," she said. "I'm so grateful to you for that, that I don't know how to tell you."

She had a little accent of some kind that I couldn't trace. It only made her all the more charming. I asked her if she were a native, and she said she wasn't, but she just loved the town and all the people and wouldn't go away now for anything. It didn't occur to me to ask her how she knew about my little duel with Sherwin; I was too in-terested in just talking to her, and she didn't seem to mind, so we kept right on without noticing that the party had thinned out until we were the last ones there and the Mahers were making noises to indicate they wanted us to go home so they could have dinner. I asked Althea if she had a date and then took her to dinner at Gaillard's and we went on with the conversation, and when the waiters there began to behave the same way the Mahers had, I brought her over here.

It must have been about one o'clock in the morning before she said she really had to go. She wanted me just to put her on a Number 7 bus, and when I just wouldn't hear of anything but taking her home in a taxi, she suddenly became very quiet, standing there on the curb. As the taxi pulled up she shook her-self just a little and said: "All right. The Ogonz Building."

After we were in the cab she said: "You see, I live there," as though it were some kind of con-fession.

I didn't see anything to be ashamed of in it; lots of those office buildings have pent-houses that have been converted into living apart-ments. But since the subject seemed to make her nervous, I said: "Can I call you there?"

It was so dark in the cab that I couldn't see her face, but her voice was quieter than ever. She said: "No. I live—a rather peculiar life, and don't have a phone."

"But when can I see you again?"

She said: "You shouldn't . . . Oh, I don't know."

I began to wonder how I'd offended her or what I'd stepped into. The suspicion even crossed my mind that she might be married or being kept by somebody, but I didn't care, I wasn't going to give up that easily. So I said: "How about Thursday, day after tomorrow? I know a little Italian restaurant where we can be quiet, and we can take in a show afterward."

She didn't say anything at all for a couple of minutes. Then she put one hand over mine and said: "I'll do it. If anything happens so that I can't make it, though, I'll leave word with Mr. Ankaiosou, the night superintendent." Then she became very gay again until we got to the building. But she wouldn't let me come up with her to the door of her apartment.

Not then nor any other time. And the more I went out with her, the better I got to know her, the more I got the impression that there was something mysterious connected with the place where she lived. She always met me downstairs, and seemed as happy as she could be to be with me, but whenever the conversation approached the subject of where and how she lived, she would suddenly go silent on me, as though it was something she didn't dare talk about. By the third or fourth time I met her I dropped any suspicion that she might be married to or living with another man. I was seeing her practically every day,

and she just couldn't have gotten away; besides, she wasn't the sort of person who would do that—too sweet and lovely and genuine.

I thought it must be because of her family or something like that, but I don't think I can really be blamed for wondering. The matter came to a head one afternoon when we were out in the park—Althea loved the park. We had been kissing and were lying on our backs on the grass, close together, not doing anything except look up through the leaves at blue sky, saying a word or two now and then.

I said to her: "Althea, why won't you ever take me home? I don't care what's the matter with it or your family. I love you."

She lifted herself up on one elbow and then bent over with her face close to mine and her hair falling down around, and said: "Dick, I love you, too, and I'll do anything you ask but that. If you come to the place where I live I'll—have to go to another, and you may not find me."

I said: "I'll have to be at the place where you live when we're married."

It was the first time I had mentioned the idea. Two big tears came out of her eyes and landed on my cheek, and then she sat up and began to cry as I have never seen anyone cry before. I was simply agonized. I tempted her out of it after a while, but the day was spoiled, and she wouldn't meet me the next day either.

After that, I let the subject of her living arrangements alone and we were happy just being together and loving each other until one day when I was at the Acme office. Sherwin was explaining that the fire inspectors had put a violation on the Ogonz Building, and that a bigger water-tank to supply the sprinkler system would have to be placed on the roof, and pointing out where it would go on the plan, when I said:

"But this plan doesn't show the pent-house."

"There isn't any pent-house on the Ogonz Building," he said. "There never was."

Now that he mentioned it, I didn't remember seeing any on the one occasion when I had visited the place. All my old suspicions and a lot of new ones came into my mind with a rush, and I decided that anything was better than this uncertainty. I had a date with Althea that evening, so I went down to the Ogonz Building just before the place closed for the day, and up to the top floor. All the offices there were perfectly good offices of perfectly good firms, no chance for a living apartment of any kind. Then I went up the stairs leading to the roof.

I could see through the wire-reinforced glass of the door leading out that there was a housing for the elevator machinery and a water tank on spidery legs, but certainly no pent-house visible on that side. I couldn't see through the back of the housing for the stair-well, of course, so I opened the door and stepped out and around. The sun was just setting, and there was a brisk wind that made me grab for my hat. The roof had a parapet around it about chin height. There were the ventilator heads, and there was the flagpole.

And there was Althea Dubois, walking toward me as if she had just stepped out from behind the flagpole. She looked so beautiful it hurt.

"Oh, Dick!" she said, in a kind of wail. "I warned you."

While I stood there she ran past me and down the stairs. Before I could catch her at the top floor, I heard the elevator grinding, and when I rang the bell it wouldn't answer. I had to walk down all the way and when I got to the ground floor there was no trace of Althea or of Mr. Ankaiosou either. I haven't been able to find any trace of either of them since. But I think she may be in some tree near where we were together, so I'm trying every one. I know if I find the right one, she'll come back to me.

The drinkers at Gavagan's Bar were silent for a moment. Then Keating said: "What did you say the night super's name was?"

"Ankaiosou; I think that's right."

Keating said softly. "Ancæus the Lesser was one of the Argonauts, a demigod. He's the only one about whose later life nothing is told. He was from Samos, and his specialty was navigation."

the
diamond
images

by...Robert Moore Williams

There were moments when he wondered why the people so obviously both feared and worshipped the old priest.

"TUM ELSO say to tell you—that humans come." The soft whisper from the open door penetrated slowly to Wolder's consciousness. Startled, he looked up. Then he saw that his visitor was Vannuy, whom he liked. A smile creased the leather of his face, making it gentle.

"Thank you, Vannuy," Wolder said.

"It was nothing." The native's face broke into a shy answering smile, then as silently as a green shadow, he slid out of the doorway. "They move like cats," Wolder thought. Eight years he had been here in this quiet spot where the jungle met the mountains without being able to learn how the natives could move so silently. As to the really important things that were here—

Putting out of his mind the thought of things he did not understand, Wolder turned back to his work. The specimen he was carefully packing for shipment had wings the color of pure gold. He slid it into its envelope and sealed the edges. The next specimen had iridescent wings. Looking at them, he felt again the old awe he had always known at the mystery of the color in

Few writers have contributed as much to the stature of Science Fiction as Robert Moore Williams, who returns with this story of a forest on Venus, which may remind you of the quiet valleys in Tibet that you've perhaps read of, where you hear the sound of temple bells in the far away distance.

the wings of a butterfly. Such beauty was here as to leave the soul of man in silent wonder, such color as to transport the eye, and such organization of dots and lines as to leave gasping the intelligence which sought for the purpose behind it. That there was *purpose* extending from the caterpillar through the butterfly Wolder did not doubt, though it might not be conceivable to the mind of man. Looking at the ugly caterpillar, all legs and bristle and ungainly movements, who could guess that this clumsy creature was destined to flit on the wings of the wind through the aisles of the jungle, to sip nectar from orchids as beautifully colored as it was?

Wolder loved butterflies. On Earth, there were collectors who paid fancy prices for the winged beauties of Venus, thus enjoying in their imagination the delights of living in the fairy jungle from which the butterflies came. Here he had lived for eight years, collecting, making friends with the natives who had built the strange temple up above him. Or was this temple actually so extraordinary a laboratory as to be inconceivable as such? What the temple was, Wolder did not know. At times he had entertained strange ideas about it, fantasies that old Tum Elso, who ruled it, who looked like a tottering beanpole and a blithering idiot, but who was utter and absolute lord of a domain that stretched for many miles through this jungle, was actually a super-scientist, and that he had at his command powers that human scientists had not yet dreamed existed. That the natives of this region feared and almost worshipped Tum Elso, Wolder well knew. However he and the native high priest were very good friends and each respected and cherished the other. Often in the cool of the evening Tum Elso came to sip scalding hot tea with him.

The clatter of hard heels on stone reminded Wolder of Tum Elso's message. "So soon?" he thought. He knew that men were coming. Only humans could walk like this, with hard ringing heels announcing their self-importance. Or perhaps their eagerness? Why should anyone be eager to see him? However, he would be happy to see them. It would be good to hear the old forgotten words again and to roll them on his tongue as he talked.

The man who appeared in the doorway was tall and clean-limbed. Clad in a jungle suit, he was wearing a plastic helmet. His face was oddly familiar, Wolder thought. Where had he seen those gray eyes before? At this moment, the man's face was twisted by some psychic tension. Shoving his helmet back, thrusting out his hand, he stepped forward.

"Hello, Dad. I was afraid you wouldn't remember me." The words were spoken wistfully as though some secret fear had been realized.

Wolder took a step backward. He was too busy looking at the pictures in his mind to notice the outstretched hand. They started from the babyhood of this man and they extended onward into his teens, cutting off eight years previously when he had left Earth. Mixed with these pictures were others, of the boy's mother. All were trying to crowd into consciousness at once.

"Dick!" Wolder whispered. This was a moment he had never expected to live to enjoy. When he had come here, he had been sure he was telling his son and his wife good-bye forever. She had been one of the reasons he had come to Venus. Ignoring the outstretched hand, he moved forward to take in his arms a son who was bigger than he was. "Your mother?" he remembered to ask at last.

"She entertained a five-star general last week," Dick answered, embarrassed. "The week before it was the captain of the Sky Queen, just in from Mars."

"Ah. The social whirl. That sort of thing always had an appeal for her." The tone of the butterfly collector's voice said this subject was closed, forever. "But what are you doing here?"

"Field expedition," the youth answered, proudly but diffidently. "I'm an archeologist. I had the good luck to hook up with an expedition coming here who needed my specialty."

"How did you reach this spot?"

"Walked. Our ship landed on the table land up above. Dad—"

"Did you get permission from Tum Elso to land here?"

"No. Didn't know it was necessary. As a matter of fact, Mr. Carnahan had the landing site all picked out before we left Earth. Dad— I'd like you to meet Sophia."

Wolder realized now that two people had entered. Looking, he saw that the other one had removed his helmet. A woman, bright and young, but with bitter lines on her jaw, stood there. Just looking at his son, Wolder knew that the youth was head over heels in love with her. He felt glad about that, but a little uncertain too.

"It is a privilege to meet you, Sophia." Wolder was confused. He turned to his son for an explanation. "Your—ah."

Divining his meaning, Dick blushed to his ears. "No. Not yet, that is." The blush deepened as he realized what he was saying. "I mean—"

"We're just good friends," the girl said, laughing. In Wolder's grasp, her hand was cool and distant, not warm and friendly as he had expected.

"Sit down, both of you, while I prepare tea."

"Tea must be frightfully expensive here," the girl protested.

"This is made from local herbs. I couldn't afford Earth tea." He did not add that he had given Dick's mother every dollar of a modest fortune before leaving Earth, setting up part of it in a tight trust fund for Dick, that she could not touch.

The girl helped him when it was

time to pour. Neither she nor Dick could repress wry grimaces at the taste of the drink. "Do tell me about your work here, Mr. Wolder," the girl said quickly. "You collect butterflies, do you not?"

Wolder found himself talking about his work, a subject that could absorb him for hours.

"Tell us about the natives," the girl questioned. "We saw some kind of a building as we came down the mountain. What was that?"

"Their temple."

Interest kindled in her eyes. "Could we see the inside?"

Wolder shook his head. "We would have to get permission." He wanted to talk about butterflies and look at his son.

"You could get permission for us, I'm sure," Sophia said.

"I doubt it. I've never been inside it myself."

"But you've been here eight years." The girl's voice was suddenly sharp.

"I've never been inside the temple."

"Why not? I should think you would be curious."

"It is a matter of waiting to be invited. I am a guest here."

The expression in the girl's eyes said she did not believe him.

Dick, squirming, spoke. "Mr. Carnahan asked us to inquire. He's in charge of the expedition. We're going to study this whole area from every possible viewpoint and we're interested in everything." His eagerness showed on his face as he talked.

He was young and the world was filled with wonder. Noticing this, Wolder sighed to himself. He had been this way once too, but time had laid its trap and he had fallen into it, somehow.

"I do not know what is in the temple," the butterfly collector answered. "However, here is a sample of native art." Lifting the lid of a chest, he took out the statuette that Tum Elso had given him, a figure about four inches tall, of a man studying a butterfly. Carved of some clear substance that reflected the light, it was perfect in form, line, and color.

"It's you!" Dick said, startled. "A perfect likeness. The person who carved that stone was a real artist!" He saw the art work, the form, the line, and the color that were present. The girl saw something else.

"It's a diamond!" she gasped. "A carved diamond, four inches tall!"

"Surely not!" Wolder said, surprised.

"It definitely is!" A touch of hysteria had appeared in her voice. "Where did you get it?"

"Tum Elso gave it to me."

"Gave it to you?" Her tones showed complete disbelief, then as she looked again at the butterfly collector, she knew he was incapable of telling a lie. Abruptly she got to her feet. "Come, Richard. It's time to return to the ship."

The youth protested. "After all, Sophia, this is the first chance I have had—"

"You can talk to him tomorrow." She flung the words back over her shoulder as she went out the door. Apologetically, Richard followed her. Wolder stifled his protests. His own feelings he could keep to himself. He was drinking tea and trying to compose his emotions when a shadow appeared in the doorway.

"Tum Elso!" Wolder rose to his feet and bowed with real pleasure. "You honor me. Enter and honor me further by drinking tea with me."

The native high priest—ruler, king, whatever the proper title was—entered and bowed in reply. Tall, his face grave and composed, his eyes thoughtful, he laid aside his staff and sat upon the floor. "You are kind." The words were in the dialect of this district, which Wolder understood as well as any human could ever expect to grasp the meaning of a language that contained only modulated tones, with no break between the words. His eyes came to rest on the statuette sitting on the small table. As if he saw things that were not visible to the ordinary eye, he seemed to muse upon it. He took the cup of tea that Wolder offered him.

"The girl who was here said it is made of diamond. Is that correct?"

"Yes." Tum Elso answered as if he had not heard. His eyes had found another object, a caterpillar that had entered the room and was crawling up the leg of a chair. Seeming to forget Wolder, and everything else, the native gave the insect his entire attention. The movements of the caterpillar began to change. It seemed to be searching, frantically, for something. Moving out on a rung of the chair, it attached itself there. Under Wolder's eyes, it began to spin a cocoon. Driven by some desperate need for haste, it worked very rapidly. A process that normally would have taken hours was ended in a few minutes. A complete cocoon was formed.

As Wolder watched, with bated breath, the cocoon split. A new insect emerged that was not a caterpillar. Stiff and sticky, it climbed up on the rung of the chair, sprouted wings, and became a butterfly. Rising in the air, it floated away.

"You—you did that!" Wolder gasped.

"I?" Tum Elso's eyes were as guileless as those of a child. "Every minute caterpillars turn into butterflies."

"But they don't do it that fast," Wolder pointed out. "You speeded up the life processes by some kind of mental force which you concentrated on the caterpillar." His voice was tight with excitement. He had seen a minor miracle and he knew it. He also knew he might never be able to prove it.

"Perhaps some freak of nature—" Tum Elso said, smiling.

"No!" Wolder shouted, then, remembering he was host here, recalled his manners and apologized. "If it was a freak, you made it into that."

Tum Elso's eyes were still as guileless as those of a child. "Who can say why and how things happen? But this was not the purpose of my visit. I came to warn you that trouble comes."

"Trouble?" The butterfly collector faltered over the word. "How do you know?"

The native priest shrugged. "Perhaps I smell it in the wind. Just keep this near you and you will come to no harm." He pointed at the statuette, then went out of the door and into the jungle world out there as silently as a green shadow.

Wolder was left to face his own troubled mind. There was regret in him. He had known peace here, and now, he suspected, it was going away. But there was happiness too, a kind of giddy joy. His son had come to him. Suddenly angry footsteps were pounding on the stones outside. He went to the doorway to face that son. The youth's face was a mixture of white and red. Anger and shame and hurt were deep within him.

"She double-crossed me. I loved her, and she told me she loved me, but she was Carnahan's woman all the time!"

"Oh!" To some degree, Wolder felt his son's pain. He hunted for words to say, knowing there were none.

"She played me for a sucker from the beginning. She and Carnahan deliberately arranged to meet me on Earth and to offer me a job as an archeologist."

"In Heaven's name, what for?" Wolder said. He was really startled.

"You were the reason." The youth's voice was hot with anger. "The whole expedition was aimed at you, and through you, at this!" His finger pointed at the statuette. "They say that whole temple is full of diamonds like that one. They brought me here to influence you enough to get them into that temple."

"The devil!" Wolder said. In a sudden flash, he saw the whole situation. Here in this peace he had forgotten that such duplicity existed and that the conquest of space had only made some men into bigger wolves without civilizing them in the least.

"When Sophia saw that diamond, she knew all she wanted to know. She dashed back to report to Carnahan. They've got men around the temple now and Carnahan and Sophia are on their way here after you. If you want to save the statuette, and your own life, you had better get out of sight."

"We'll do that," Wolder said, sweeping the statuette into his pocket. "You come with me. There are places to hide here where we will never be found." He started toward the back, then stopped as he realized his son was not following him.

"You're not coming." Wolder broke off as he saw the expression on Dick's face. "Don't tell me that you still love that girl!" His voice was sharp with pain and reproof.

"I—I guess I do," Dick said,

miserably. "Carnahan has her in his control and she's in a spot where she needs help. I thought I'd warn you, then go back and see what I could do."

"My son, my son," Wolder whispered.

"She actually hasn't had a real chance," the youth pled. "Her old man was a drunken bum and she ran away from home when she was fifteen. I thought that maybe here—" His wish, and hidden dream, were left unspoken as the sound of running feet came from outside. A shot sounded there.

In the doorway, Vannuy collapsed and died.

As Wolder moved toward the native, the doorway was darkened again by a big man that he knew intuitively was Carnahan. Heavy jowls stuck out on either side of the space man's face as he glared into the cabin. A Zen gun was at the ready in his hands. Behind him, also armed, was Sophia. Excitement was on her face, and defiance, but the defiance was directed at something inside of her, not outside.

"Are you Wolder?" Carnahan said. Without waiting for an answer, he continued. "Come on. You're helping us get into that temple up the slope." He did not comment on Richard's presence here.

"I am not!" Wolder said. He was surprised and pleased that he had the strength to stand up to this man. "These people here are my friends. I would not rob them for the sake of a ruffian at the head of a crew of murderers."

The collector's words were vehement. They left him a little dazed. He had not known he was capable of such statements. Carnahan needed a moment to realize he was being defied. In the silence that followed, Wolder heard his son whisper, "At a time, Dad!" In the eyes of the girl, as she looked at him with a new respect, there was a sudden hunger as if she was seeing something that she wanted.

Carnahan shifted the Zen gun. "I'll put a bullet in you."

"How will I help you if I am dead?"

On the space man's face, the jowls hardened and thickened. Abruptly he swung the muzzle of the weapon to point at Richard.

Wolder cried out in sudden anguish. The youth faced the gun without faltering. "Go on and shoot, you dog. I'm not afraid to die."

In this moment, Wolder was very proud of his son. But he was afraid too and he cried out. "No. I'll show you all I know."

"That's better," Carnahan said, lowering the weapon.

Wolder walked beside his son up the slope. Neither looked back. A dozen men from the ship surrounded the big dome-shaped temple. It was made of stone, and so far as the collector knew, it had only one entrance, a heavy door made of some metal that looked like copper.

"Just get the door open," Carnahan ordered. "We'll do the rest."

As he spoke, the door opened. Tum Elso, a trace of a smile on his bland face, stood there. He bowed to Wolder.

"My friend, you honor me. Come in." As he spoke, the high priest bowed again. "And your friends too."

Wolder spoke so rapidly he almost babbled. "These are not my friends. They are robbers. They mean to steal everything you have."

A growl came from Carnahan as he spoke but Tum Elso's face did not lose any of its blandness. "Then they will be doubly interested in what we have here." The gesture to enter was inviting and unmistakable.

"Hold it," the space man spoke. "I don't like this. It may be a trap. You, Sophia, stay out here with half the men. I'll take the others inside. If there is any sign of anything crooked, you come shooting." Taking the lead, he stepped through the door, then stopped, a cry of amazed wonder on his lips.

Following, Wolder saw that the interior of this huge hollow half shell was illumined by some kind of light which came from no visible source but which seemed to be a part of the very air in here. It penetrated the entire interior of the vast chamber. He also saw why Carnahan had cried out in wonder.

Narrow partitions of some clear substance running from roof to floor made the whole vast chamber into a huge honeycomb. The partitions were broken into cells about five inches in height. In each of the cells was a glittering statuette similar to the one he had in his pocket, except that they were models of natives. There were thousands of them. Each one reflected back the light in a myriad of sparkling beams so that the whole room was filled with their glitter.

A single grunted word came from Carnahan's throat. "Diamonds!" He snatched a statuette from the nearest cell. A jeweler's eye-piece came out of his pocket and went into his eye. When he looked up again, he was gasping for breath. "It *is* a diamond. They all are. Sophia wasn't lying." For a moment, the thought of the wealth that was in his possession held his entire attention. During this moment, the jowls on his face worked like those of a hog at a swill trough. Then his eyes came to Wolder. "Ask him where he got 'em."

"I made them," Tum Elso replied to the question.

Carnahan gulped at this idea. It was almost too big even for his appetite.

"Ask him if he would like to see the new batch I am just finishing, and the process," the high priest said to Wolder.

Carnahan's jowls worked again as he tried to swallow what he was seeing in his own mind. The content was too big for him, he could not get it down, nor could he reject it. For an instant he stood with his throat bulging, then with a mighty effort, he made up his mind. "Tell him to show me!" he snarled. "But tell him to go first. I'm not turning my back to any native."

Completely ignoring the Zen gun at his back, the high priest led the way to the front of the big temple. What was there looked like a large vat filled with some kind of oily liquid. Although it was black, this liquid seemed to be sparkling with millions of points of exploding light. Looking at it, Wolder did not doubt that it was radioactive. Tum Elso moved to the end of the vat and pressed a lever there. Movement began in the dark liquid. A submerged platform rose. It was covered with glittering statuettes.

"Force fields in the liquid cause the atoms to form around a pattern that is laid down from my own mind," Tum Elso said to Wolder. Or this was what the collector thought he said. Actually he was not paying much attention to the high priest. His entire mind was concentrated on the images.

The whole crew of the space ship was there, as statuettes. Wolder saw Sophia, and his own son.

"That's me!" Carnahan whispered, pointing to one of the images. He turned suspicious eyes on Tum Elso. Abruptly the Zen gun came up. "Ask him why he made an image of me? What kind of a trick is this?"

"He—he thought you would be pleased to have a diamond statuette of you," Wolder hastily said. "It—it's a present." He tried to hide his confusion and to make the words both meaningful and flattering.

What the high priest had seemed to say was, "These men are the caterpillars and the images are the butterflies." This had no meaning, to Wolder, at this point, and he had no time to think of a possible meaning.

"A present, huh." Carnahan looked pleased. Some of the fear went out of his eyes. But not all of it. This image worried him. It was as if he, the vital part of him, was sitting on the platform from which the oily liquid was slowly and reluctantly draining. His mind turned and twisted as he sought a meaning. The fear in him was being held in check by the thought of a present. "How does he do it? It's like making a picture of you when you're not there."

"He says he can make such a picture of anybody, anywhere," Wolder translated.

"Hunh?" Carnahan twisted this answer around in his mind and tried to make sense of it, but failed. "I guess it don't matter how he does it, just so he can do it. Marsdon, go outside and get those sacks we brought from the ship. We're going to start getting this stuff out of here."

Marsdon was tall, with a face like a ferret. A grin on the ferret face, he went on a lope for the outside. Like his leader, he was seeing what these images would buy for him. He would have a never-ending drunken spree in all the space ports of the system.

Marsdon came back into the temple as quickly as he had left it. The grin was gone from his ferret face. As he walked toward the front, he took quick glances over his shoulder as though he thought that someone, or something, was following invisibly behind him.

"What the hell is wrong with you?" Carnahan demanded.

The ferret face formed a grimace as Marsdon tried to look, but no words came. He jerked his head over his shoulder. "Out there. Go look."

Carnahan glanced at Tum Elso. The high priest's eyes were again as guileless as those of a child. Moving to the big door, he looked out. Wolder, following, did not believe his eyes.

Sophia, clutching her Zen gun, was standing just outside the door, frozen statue-stiff. A slight jungle breeze, pressured by the coming darkness, ruffled her hair. There was no other movement anywhere about her. Behind her, a man squatted on the ground. Like the girl, he had a Zen gun ready, and also like her, he looked as if he would never use it. One man was watching the clearing. A jungle lion could spring upon him and he would never see the beast. The others stood in similar frozen poses.

"Sophia!" Carnahan shouted.

There was no answer. The space man shouted again, a bull roar that set the echoes ringing. The girl did not stir.

Slowly the space man turned back into the room. Tum Elso had followed and was standing directly behind him. The high priest held the statuette of Carnahan in his hands. Wolder saw that all the others in the room were also suddenly frozen, including his son.

"You are in trouble?" Tum Elso said, to Carnahan. His voice was soft. Only the slightest overtone showed the deadly menace in it.

Carnahan tried to lift the Zen gun. It would not come up. Some vast force seemed to be slowing, or prohibiting, every movement the space man tried to make. Wolder did not doubt what would happen if Carnahan ever got the gun up. The explosive slugs would blast the life from Tum Elso.

"Damn you—" The words seemed to come from some well of agony within Carnahan. His voice went into strained, taut silence. Deep down inside he was trying to speak but the force was now holding his vocal chords, preventing all sound.

The whole vast honey-comb temple was still. In every cell, the statuettes seemed to be waiting, for something. While they waited, they cringed. Carnahan was now a frozen statue too.

Holding the little statuette of the space man in front of him, the high priest let it slide from his fingers.

Striking the floor, it burst into a thousand glittering fragments.

Carnahan's body burst into similar fragments. Blood in a fine spray, bits of flesh, and fragments of bone exploded outward from what had been a man. Carnahan did not fall.

There was not enough of him left to fall. He went into fragments too small for this. Only the Zen gun fell, striking the floor with a metallic clatter.

"Robber! Killer! Space wolf come to roam in the jungle!" Tum Elso's words had the finality of a doom that was already accomplished. Reaching into the pocket of the robe that he wore, he pulled out another statuette, that of Marsdon. The high priest flung the little image against the wall where it burst into fragments. Marsdon went the same way that Carnahan had gone. The bits of flesh and bone that remained would never swagger, drunk, with a girl on each arm, down the main streets of the space ports of the system. Again Tum Elso's hand went into the robe. Seeing the statuette that he brought out this time, Wolder cried out in sudden protest.

"No! No!"

Surprised, the high priest looked at him, and held the arm that was about to throw.

"That is my son!" Wolder whispered. Such agony was in him as he had never known existed.

Surprise deepened on the face of the high priest. "My friend, I did not know this." A touch of sympathy came over the features, then was gone in a rising sternness. "But even if he is your son, he is here with killers and would-be robbers!"

Words clamored in Wolder's throat, and stuck there. He forced them out. "But he did not know

what they were when he came. As soon as he learned, he left them, and came to warn me. We were starting to hide when we were caught."

Tum Elso hesitated, the sternness melted, then came back. "Here we are known by the kind of wolf pack we run with."

"But he is different."

As if he had not heard, the high priest continued. "The only way I can keep peace in this jungle is because the wolves know what will happen if they show their teeth." His hand swept up to indicate the thousands of glittering statuettes in their cells. "Each one there knows me, and fears me, and keeps my peace because he knows his image is here. This is the only language wolves understand."

"But he is not a wolf."

"Of course, you will say that, because he is your son. Why should I treat him differently than the others?" Again the hand went up as if to throw the statuette against the stone wall.

Wolder did not quite know how he did it, but he instantly stooped and picked up Carnahan's Zen gun. He pointed it at Tum Elso. "This is one reason," he said. Sweat was on his face and running down into his eyes and he did not care.

"I am your friend," the high priest spoke. "Would you shoot *me?*"

Wolder felt as if the sweat was seeping down into his soul. He had known peace here in this place, but what he had not known was that this high priest had kept this peace, nor the means that had been used. "If I have to, I will shoot you," he whispered.

Tum Elso folded his arms. His face was granite-hard. "What would you have me do, my one-time friend? If I turn these robbers loose, they will come again."

Wolder shook his head. "After you show them what has happened here, and after I tell them what you can and will do, they will tuck their tails between their legs and not stop running until they reach the other side of Earth's moon."

"Um." The flicker of a grin split the granite of Tum Elso's face as he thought about this, then was gone. "And your son? What would you have me do with him?"

"I would have you keep him here with me, him—and the girl."

"What?" Thunder was in the sing-song voice. "To breed a pack of wolf puppies in the doorway of my temple?"

"It will not be that way," Wolder said. "Let them live here and know the meaning of peace and the wolf strain will die out. The girl has good stuff in her. I saw it in the way she looked at me when I defied Carnahan. And my son loves her."

"There is no loyalty and no honor in her."

"There will be. That I promise you."

"And if I do not do what you wish?"

Wolder made a slight movement with the Zen gun. For what seemed a long time, Tum Elso stared at the weapon, then his eyes went from it to the man behind it.

"And if I do what you wish, what guarantee do I have that your promise will be kept?"

"This," Wolder said. Reaching into his pocket, he took out his own statuette, which he handed to Tum Elso.

The high priest stared at it. When he spoke his voice was very soft. "You give me this, knowing what I can do with it?"

"Yes," Wolder answered.

Lights glinted in Tum Elso's eyes. Or were they tears? His voice was softer still. "Before such faith as you have, and before the action you have just taken, I am powerless, my friend again. It shall be as you wish." The smile on his face was like a benediction in this room of glittering statuettes. From each gleaming facet in a thousand diamond images, the reflected light seemed suddenly to take on all the colors of a rainbow.

As night came on, Wolder sat at his bench working with his beloved butterflies. The ship, with its dazed and frightened crew, had long since blasted into the sky. Outside, he could hear his son and Sophia talking. The girl was still in a state of shock, but she was coming out of it. The core of decency and honesty that Wolder had sensed under her hard surface was also coming to the fore. This showed in her voice, which sounded as if for the first time in her life, she was finding out the meaning of happiness. Hearing this, the butterfly collector was content.

Then the voices outside went into quick silence as Tum Elso entered.

"You are a very brave man, my friend," the high priest said. "Because of this, I give your life, and that of the others, into your own keeping."

On the bench in front of the startled Wolder, he set three gleaming statuettes.

"No, no. Do not thank me," Tum Elso continued, before Wolder could speak. The gesture of his hand indicated the two who were outside. "They are caterpillars now. One day they will be butterflies. It is for this day that old ones such as you, and I, must live—and dream."

"Yes!" Wolder whispered, in answer.

NEXT ISSUE—

now

the

nonterrestrial

by . . . Ivan T. Sanderson

What should an intelligent being from outside our solar system look like and have any visited this planet?

THERE has been a great deal of talk throughout history and, it would seem, since early prehistoric times about the presence in our midst of intelligent beings that, for some reason, were considered not to be indigenous to this earth. Stone Age artists depicted monstrous-looking beings of humanoid type which they appear to have regarded as supernatural or at least unnatural and quite distinct from mere foreigners from other lands, on the one hand, and from gods on the other. Almost all if not entirely all religions affirm in their early formative periods the existence of beings both superior and in some respects — though mostly morally— inferior but nonetheless intelligent, which are alleged to be out of this world. Primitive monotheists such as the Semitic respecters of *Yahweh,* the Zoroastrians, the West African animists, and even the Australoid tribesmen, from the first, asserted that there were intermediaries between their miserable selves and the Almighty—superior beings but not themselves gods nor any more the "sons of God" than are men. The great teachers, from the prophets of Sumeria and Ancient Egypt to the

Ivan T. Sanderson, who has been interested in Ufology for many years, continues his challenging series of articles in which he explores possible explanations of the phenomena. He is the author of numerous books including the recent MONKEY KINGDOM *and* LIVING MAMMALS OF THE WORLD *(Hanover House).*

Gautama Buddha, Christ, and even Mohammed, affirmed the same. The Angels were the *Messengers* of God; plain straightforward folk like us, different only in that they had had longer to learn the ways of the Almighty—ways that can only result in greater intelligence, purity, and understanding.

Sweep away all the dross of ethics and morals and other irksome disciplines devised by and necessary for a life-form (such as ourselves) struggling up from unknowingness, through stupidity, to some enlightened understanding of things, and much of the alleged mystical pronouncements of the ancients don't look quite so puerile. Even the matter of devils becomes less lugubrious and if you will reread what is written about these characters you will note that, although they are credited with all manner of malevolence and almost a corner in evil, they appear as not really evil themselves, but just wicked and profoundly different. The Devil is a bogeyman to us but to the ancients he had a lighter side, and a darned efficient organization too, if we are to believe the early scribes.

These are very basic religious questions that do not further concern us except to demonstrate that throughout the ages there has been a persistent acceptance—rather than a mere belief—that there are in existence more enlightened and competent beings than our own kind and that they don't dwell here habitually, but come down here out of the sky,

and seem—as we say today—not to have been evolved here.

The gamut of these types is, however, rather extensive and is not confined to mere godlets, angels, devils, and humanoid messengers, but has always included also a considerable galaxy of *Little Folk* such as fairies, pixies, and similar entities called throughout the world by all manner of names such as *dwendies,* in Central America, and *chongolis* in inner China. (It would seem that the "—is" sound almost universally denotes smallness). These little ones have never been regarded as particularly decent or indecent, holy or evil, but to be either a nuisance or mysteriously magnanimous though always aloof, unpredictable, and altogether "not-of-us." While human beings have sometimes readily given themselves to the devil and always stood in utter awe of the Angels, they seem never to have known quite what to do about the little folk. Basically, men have always seemed scared stiff of them and, failing to be able to please them either by good deeds or bad, have just put out little bowls of honey for them and hoped for the best.

Then again, there is another mysterious fact about history. If you dig back to the earliest records of any nation or tribal group you will invariably come up against the statement, in one form or another that "In the beginning there came to our country *men* who taught us . . . etc." And the emphasis here is on the word *Men*. These were never aileged to be gods or even super-beings but plain, straightforward earthly men—though usually pale-skinned, with beards, having ships and clothes, and knowing about agriculture and building in stone. The statement itself is a contradiction in terms because if *people came*, there were people there already, and those who came must have come from somewhere else and been *there* already. Professor William James Perry of Liverpool University in his remarkable book *The Growth of Civilization*, (1924, Dutton, New York) has sought to show—and not, indeed, without great cogency—that all these people who *came* to other lands throughout the world were the descendants of those first people who discovered that plants gave rise to seeds which, when planted gave rise to more plants and thus discovered agriculture (probably on the banks of one of the great rivers flowing through the northern deserts, such as the Nile, that bring floods once a year) and thus founded settled civilization. His belief is that they spread slowly all over the earth, carrying with them this novel idea of *planting* food instead of collecting it, and the concommitant ideas of village life, stone buildings, astronomy, religion such as we know it, metallurgy, boating, and all the rest.

Professor Perry may have something here or he may have become over-enthusiastic, but that is really beside the point, which is that these people who *came* to other lands in turn asserted universally they did not invent these useful processes themselves, but that *they* "got them from the gods." This may have been only a polite form of diplomacy or an easy way out of awkward questions, but then, tracing these Children of the Sun back to their original *mastaba* tombs, megalithic monuments, and other early evidences of what we call civilization, we run smack into a real problem. Where is the enormously long period of evolution needed to evolve the very things they seem to have possessed? It simply is not there in the archaeological record.

If the Children of the Sun were missionaries from the first center of established civilization, wherever that may have been, they would seem to have appeared first in those very river valleys mentioned above —the Nile, Tigris-Euphrates, and Indus; and possibly the Ganges, Brahmaputra, the Yangtse-Kiang, though the last three did not flood annually—bringing with them their full blown and highly advanced culture. As to where they came from we do not know though all sorts of suggestions have been made. For instance, the Dynastic Egyptians were once thought to have come from the Hadramaüt in southern Arabia. The only practical suggestion, however, seems to be the one that is most frowned upon; namely, that they came from some lands that lay in the central Atlantic and that they were the last wave of peoples to leave those lands as they gradually sank, starting in 25,000 B.C. when their fisherfolk quit and landed on the western fringes of Europe—the Cro-Magnons — and continuing in the form of the Magdalenians, the Azilians, and Capsians, and finally the Iberians. The idea is that the leaders or most civilized communities from the cultural center of those sinking lands left last, in ships, and fanned out all over the world. Those who believe in this theory used to assert that "civilization" was discovered and slowly developed in those lands, over an immense period of time, and "ending" about 8000 B.C. when the last land sank in a cataclysm, a tradition of which lingered in the writings of the Greek, Plato. However, the practitioners who reached other lands, always insisted that they got *their* knowledge from outsiders.

This is an irksome question that stampedes all scientists and thoroughly alarms the average person. Yet, it is by no means as bad as something much more concrete that has come up recently and which has been not only talked about but also most heartily endorsed by certain scientists, technicians, historians, government officials, and others of like standing and of altogether acceptable orthodox scientific training. The problem was succinctly summarized in a radio broadcast discussion in the Sunday series entitled *The Georgetown University Forum* that has been maintained over a radio station in Washington, D. C., by Georgetown University for many years and which is most widely and universally respected for its high intellectual integrity and scientific accuracy. To summarize briefly, this is the pith of what was then said.*

Some years ago a Mr. Arlington H. Mallery, a retired engineer, became interested in some ancient maps discovered by a Turkish naval officer in Istanbul and presented to our Library of Congress. These maps were drawn at about the time of Columbus but were stated to have been copies of very much more ancient maps that were customarily used by mariners for centuries before that time, and which, in fact, stemmed from maps compiled by the Alexandrine Greeks and other eastern Mediterraneans in Roman times, again, in accord with even earlier maps stemming from Ancient Egypt and/or other still earlier civilizations. The maps had been considered interesting museum pieces but were neglected, stored, and forgotten. Mr. Mallery was led to them through his many years of research into ancient iron artifacts in America, other evidences of a Pre-Amerindian race in North America, and of the very great changes in our shore and coastlines since the retreat of the last Ice Advance (now known, from radio-carbon dating, to have occurred only about 10,000 years ago). He had heard that there were ancient maps

*Reprints of transcripts of this program are available from that station and make some of the most extraordinary reading of anything that has been published in this century. It is the standing of the participants in that discussion which lends the whole thing its startling aspects.

in existence that, though made in Europe or Asia, showed the American coastline.

When he rediscovered these—now called the Piri Reis Maps—he found that, while landmasses were depicted out in and beyond the great oceans that were shown as surrounding the main continent of Eurasia, they looked to be purely imaginary lands. Besides, even the "known" world centered around the Mediterranean, was all cockeyed; yet, when he examined the details, he found to his astonishment that by going slowly along any coast from some known point (like the township of Marseilles, that was on both these ancient and modern maps, and which has existed for centuries and not moved its position) every little promontory, inlet and island was there and *in the right order* but *out of position*. It was, Mr. Mallery tells me, just as if the original mapmakers had charted the whole coastline of the world accurately but then lacked any concept of latitude or longitude and so had no way of transferring their linear discoveries on to a two-dimensional surface. At first, in fact, he considered the possibility that the original draftsmen might have thought the earth to be flat; but, even adjusting for this idea, he still found the relative positions of all recognizable points to be altogether inaccurate and, in fact, perfectly whacky. Then he noticed something else—namely, that they were all *equally* whacky in certain particular mathematical respects. This could only

mean one thing and was a very great discovery, for it showed that these cartographers *did* use some kind of what is called a *grid* on which to plot their charted details. What was this grid?

To make a long story short, Mr. Mallery went to work with Mr. M. I. Walters, of the U. S. Hydrographic Office, and after much patient research, they found a grid that fitted the maps. They then *corrected* the maps from that grid to one of our own modern projections and something altogether amazing emerged.

These ancient maps—the originals from which they had been copied dated at the latest 3000 B.C.—showed the *entire world* in great detail and absolute accuracy and included not only the coastlines of the Americas but also that of the entire Antarctic, and, in addition, displayed a plethora of mountain ranges in the middle of all the great land-masses that most accurately depicted not only those we know but numbers of others in certain unexplored regions of northern North America and in Antarctica that we did not know—the latter in places that are now covered with a continuous, smooth dome of ice estimated to be almost two miles thick! Only in some limited areas did the coastlines *not* coincide with modern maps but it was this very fact that most startled Mr. Mallery, for some of these were spots covered by his previous researches into changing coastlines, and in each case the old maps coincided with his findings. In other words, they showed where the coast-lines should have been seven to ten thousand years ago according to his findings from quite other sources. Then Mr. Walters made another most remarkable and chance discovery.

Going over certain U. S. Army maps—or rather surveys—that had just been completed in northern Canada and its great arctic islands and which had not been published, since these lands had never before been mapped, he found to his amazement that whole mountain ranges had come to light that had until then (1952) been quite unknown to the modern world, but all of which were on these ancient Piri Reis maps and *in the right places* and of the right shape, size, and orientation. Greatly mystified, he and Mr. Mallery then went to the Reverend Daniel Linehan, S. J., Director of Weston Observatory of Boston College, Chief Seismologist to the U. S. Navy IGY explorations in Antarctica, and showed him all the mountain ranges and the coastlines in that continent, shown on the ancient maps. Almost unbelievingly, Father Linehan states on the broadcast named above that one and all of these physical features that have subsequently been investigated by scientific depth-soundings made through the ice by Task Force 43, have proved to exist just as shown on the Piri Reis maps.

Now this poses a question indeed. Who was boating all around the American continents and Antarctica *before* the ice-cap formed on the latter, and who penetrated the inner recesses of northern Canada and its great islands at that time?

You can't beg the question and say that the maps were made only at the time of Columbus because, first, the Americas, let alone Antarctica, were unknown at that time and, second, if they had been known they would already have been covered with ice so that said mountains and coastlines would not have been available for charting. As the learned but admittedly mystified gentlemen on that program confessed, the thing defies comprehension unless (1) there were expert surveyors and cartographers with very precise instruments who knew that the world was a globe drifting in space, before 3000 B.C. and (2) these personages (or beings) had not only most seaworthy ships *but also flying devices of some sort*, for, it was their express belief that those inland mountain ranges could not have been mapped so accurately by even the best equipped teams travelling over the surface of the earth.

Here is a pretty one! This is not a science-fiction story, believe me; nor is it a report on some theory developed by some hard-working individual with a mission, either erudite and sound, or uneducated and mystic. It is a sober report by top-notch Government-paid technical scientists of the highest probity, and made public withal on a respected radio broadcast in our national capital. There is no question of trickery or fakery here. The maps are genuine; there for all to see; and have been in the safekeeping of our Congress for years. These findings cannot be denied. They have got to be explained, and there is only one possible explanation—namely, shortly after the retreat of the last Ice Advance, or shift in the whole earth's crust, which moved, among other things, that part of the land we call the Great Lakes area out from under the North Pole, there were intelligent creatures on this planet who had some kind of airplanes, most advanced surveying instruments, and a knowledge of tridimensional geography that beats ours. Who were these beings, where did they come from, and where did they go?

The whole business, of course, conflicts in every way with all the findings of anthropology, archaeology, and history. Despite the four ice-advances during the immediately past few hundred thousand years, a fairly continuous and orderly evolution of both human beings and their artifacts leading to civilization has been unearthed all over the world. True, there are some nasty ones like another discovery of Dr. Mallery's (which has now been seconded by both the Smithsonian Institute and the U. S. Bureau of Standards who ran the tests) namely, that some people seven thousand years ago were also making steels in the form of alloys that require 9000° C. for their manufacture. And, who had furnaces of that nature, then? There are also these myths and traditions mentioned at the outset, first, of superior beings; then of messengers looking like us; then, of those bearded gentry who "came to our country in the first times"; and finally, of these other superior beings from whom they in turn got their knowledge of sunworship, building in stone, seamanship, etc. And all the time, there are the little pixies and fairies bobbing in and out of history apparently participating neither in our own earthly progress nor the affairs of these superior types. What are we to make of all this?

I have thought long and profoundly on this tangled skein, and I have tried to talk to all manner of people who should know about the matter but I find that people either just don't want to talk about it at all or, while expressing stunned amazement if not outright doubt, simply do not care to interpret any mystery in their own field through evidence in another field. Thus, the anthropologist will not as yet accept or even go into the evidence of the metallurgists or hydrographers, while the archaeologist won't even accept some of the findings of the anthropologist. Therefore, I cannot record *any* balanced theories and can only offer a series of my own in the form of simple equations.

There seems to be (and to have been for some time) only one intelligent life-form on this earth—*i.e.* Man, as we call him. We may find that Hominoids (that is manlike creatures) have been around a lot longer than we recently supposed

vide, the very man-like ape known as *Oreopithecus,* many bones of which have come from coal mines of the Miocene Age in Italy, in coal laid down 10 million years ago. Moreover, despite many things doubtless still to be discovered about our ancestry, we do seem to have *evolved here* and from a common ancestor with the living apes and both of us from monkey-like forebears stemming from Lemurs, and so on. The point is, there is every evidence that there has been a continuous line of ascent from the "animal" to the "intelligent," and in culture from the collecting, to the hunting, to the agricultural, to the industrial. There are funny things like this sudden appearance of the Aurignacian culture, but then sunken islands could explain this. Everything else appears to be fairly orderly and progressive. But then come along items like these damned maps, and those even more profoundly damned steel and pewter artifacts taken out of solid oolitic limestone and which could only have been sealed in there for seventy *million* years. There are, in fact, lots of things that don't fit into the orderly and "logical" time scale. The vast ruins of Ponape Island in the Pacific, and the holes bored by *marine* animals in the walls of Tiahuanaco (see Harold T. Wilkins, *Mysteries of Ancient South America*) now two miles high in Peru, don't fit at all. Phoenician cities in the Amazon Basin with inscriptions in two scripts

giving the names and dates (887-856 B.C.) of kings of Tyre and Sidon in Palestine don't figure (see L. Schwennhagen, *Antiga Historia do Brazil,* 1928); nor do over thirty thousand clay figurines including representations of one- and two-horned rhinoceroses, and of elephants, found in Guanajuato in Mexico; nor circular stone forts with steel implements in the northern Rockies; nor, above all, the circular forts of Scotland and Ireland with their granite ramparts partly melted to glass, *on their* upper edges, mark you, which is something that we cannot do except with atomic heats! Then, add to these the ancient myths and traditions of superior beings who taught our rude ancestors all these things, and of great civilizations that either died away or *went away,* and one begins to wonder. All these equations have an "x" in them and the more I have pondered this, the more I have begun to wonder whether there may not be, in truth, but a single missing factor that may replace this unknown.

It is my frank thought that there is, and that this is simply *"outside influence."*

Supposing that evolution has proceeded in an orderly manner on this planet just as the record of the rocks and our spades have shown—*vis-a-vis* our species and other earthly animals and plants, that is—there is still no reason why it should preclude other orderly evolutions elsewhere. Surely the Almighty did not confine such a process to but one planet going around one commonplace sun. Why, Nature by herself will apparently kick-off "life" on a hydrocarbon basis anywhere that there is enough water between certain temperatures, and given some time. Supposing also that not just one but sundry life forms finally attained to intelligence (whatever that may be) and got to space travel; natural curiosity alone might eventually bring them around to our watery planet. Don't forget that water is the most remarkable substance in the universe and really rather rare, so that hydrocarbon-based life-forms would naturally tend to single out water-planets first. Not just one but dozens, hundreds, thousands, hundreds of thousands, or millions of different life-forms may, in the infinity of past time, have come by here. They may have come and then gone again; they may have stayed and minded their own business, or they may have interfered; they may even have settled and colonized. If the "x" in all these conundrums that modern science is unearthing in increasing numbers, is just this factor, then we have to do a spot of reappraisal of many things. Let us start with the modern reports of "visitations" from without this earth.

These fall into four main categories: (1) Unknowns in machines —*vide*, "flying saucers" and certain other Ufos, and such entities in "space-suits" as the so-called "Flatwoods Monster" from Sutton, West Virginia (1951), (2) Disembodied entities of all kinds ranging from Poltergeists and some Ghosts to all manner of mystical entities. (3) Human or humanoid messengers or "gods" in the animistic sense, such as the Martian, Venusians, and all the other "beautiful people" of the Contacters, *plus* Angels, and the majority of "devils"—at least those that don't immediately dissolve in puffs of sulphorous vapour—, and these *Messengers* of the ancients. And, (4) the Little People, ranging from the for-some-reason so-called "Little *Green* Men" (though one and all have been reported to be aluminum-colored, though sometimes wearing green clothes) to the traditional pixies, gnomes, fairies, elfs, dwendies, chumbies, and what have you. There are also types that do not seem to fall into any one of these categories but their numbers are so few in comparison to the overwhelming historical galaxy of these four that they may be excluded and disregarded for now. Let us, then, analyze these four main types.

There is little to be said at this juncture about the first lot. Until we get one, we might as well confine our activities to recording sightings and trying to analyze the physical features and actions of their machines. Only in the very rare cases where the "pilot" has been observed outside one, should we pause to consider. I investigated one of these cases—the famed Flatwoods business—myself and very thoroughly. It is a story in itself that I would like to tell one day in this magazine, and it has some fascinating aspects that have not so far been published. The two important ones are that the machine (a pear-shaped object that glowed but which was not hot) *landed*, and something very like a modern deep-sea diving device came out of it and floated in the air like a balloon; but, more important, both this and the main machine completely *dissolved* or vaporized in a matter of forty-five minutes. This may explain many things about at least some of those Ufos that are constructions. They could come from places that are of a very different temperature to the surface of this earth or from ones that have different atmospheres so that the metals or plastics of which they are made, rapidly vaporize in our combination of oxygen, hydrogen, nitrogen, and so on. Be it noted that there were six machines flying in formation over Flatwoods when they hit an updraft of air coming from the industrial area of West Virginia and which that day was filled with impurities such as carbon monoxide and still further polluted with smog from vast forest fires further south. Many Ufos may simply not be able to land, any more than we will be able to do for a very long time under the miles deep sea of methane that is believed to cover Jupiter.

The matter of Disembodied Entities (No. 2, above) frankly alarms me. I personally am very pragmatic, being trained as a biologist. I don't like things I can't measure, put in a bottle, or skin and stuff for museum exhibit. I have not investigated any ghosts (though I have seen some pretty inexplicable things that didn't seem to have respectable *bodies* and which I like to think were all imagination, or due to a sluggish liver or bad liquor) and I have read a lot about them, but I don't propose to investigate any. This is not to deny that they can exist or that there is a vast body of reports and some evidence to substantiate their existence. Still, I cannot see what they can add to history or reality at this point, unless they are prepared to come down to earth, as it were, and give us some concrete facts with equally physical proof of the matters with which we are here concerned, in the form of, say, some more maps, a key to deciphering some writings that tell us where they grew the food to support the labor that built Ponape which is now bang-smack in the middle of a vast ocean, or something else really useful of that nature. But ghosts, spirits, and other disembodied entities have throughout the ages steadfastly refused to do anything like this. They just go on haunting and usually moaning. Perhaps, if they do exist, even without a physical existence, they are just too dumb or uneducated to know anything or even to speak. In fact, I'm not at all sure they may not be mere projections and I don't think they can add anything to our discussion.

The third type of "visitor" is quite another matter. Let us take the modern ones (post Kenneth Arnold, 1947) first. These—the "splendours" of Adamski, Menger, Betherun, *et alia,*—are not by any means uniquely a post-Arnold development. They go back to most ancient times. They all have one thing in common, namely, they *preach* rather than *teach*, and they have an extraordinary ability to appear always to be completely contemporary with the cultures to which they preach. This is very suspect but, it must be admitted, not a complete illogicality. We are starting to tamper with the bodily forms of animals (*vide,* experiments on pollywogs to get extra legs, *etc.*) and primitive tribesmen centuries ago imitated the cries of animals well enough to fool the creatures themselves. A scientist has just broken the most improbable script (see *Scientific American*, July, 1958) used by the extinct Easter Islanders, and it would be no problem to "break" the code of our language, learn it, and use it in contacting us.

If the "Angels" of the ancients were but superior beings made (and perhaps by their own surgeons) in *our* rather than God's image they might well have impressed mere men, even if they did not provide any concrete evidence of any great scientific mysteries. They might also, in time, have acquired wings on their shoulders that were really on the aerial machines they used to land on dreary deserts. Both they and their modern counterparts are certainly more interested in preaching ideas than in teaching practical science but who are we to say that the end product of knowledge may not be nothing more than ideas, and anybody who has perfected space travel must be pretty intelligent and advanced. Yet, there is a vast impracticality about these modern human-type visitors which is not compatible with that advanced intelligence—at least to our present way of thinking. Why do they persist in picking out almost the least important people to contact and ones who, however worthy, upright and reliable previously, are most likely to be disbelieved thereafter, and thus able to do least in "furthering the cause." Perhaps there is a plan in all this, and "prophets" ultimately *do* achieve more change in the long run than princes and emperors or even scientists. It is a humbling thought and I'm quite prepared to accept it, but still, I would indeed wish that these "modern angels" would drop the communist party line, write down some of their ideas, give us a few formulae (for the edification of our primitive minds), and present some evidence both of their existence and of the value and validity of their doctrines.

So then we come to devils. These I personally dig; they are so much more down to earth and practical. They *do* things (however unpleasant) rather than *preaching* pleasantries. They are warm and nasty instead of cold and aloof, and they appear to have a lot of reptilian qualities like tails, scales, and funny feet, horns, lots of teeth, and so forth. They can be attacked and beaten up if they make nasty stinks. But just where do they fit in, and can there be any logical explanation of the concept? I have heard one that seems to cover all others and it goes as follows:

Intelligent life does not have to be evolved just as it has on this earth. It could have arisen on a rather hotter planet and in a form that looks to us like (but is not, of course, genetically related to) the reptilian on this planet. These could have scales or wear scaly space-suits and have tails with a terminal spike (like our lions), horns or other head-protuberances, and what we call cloven-hoofs like our antelopes and pigs and so forth. They could even lay eggs. They might carry trident-like weapons and be naturally a bit rough and even flesh-eaters. After all, most of us are! Most important of all, they may be rather a nuisance in our part of this galaxy or in the universe generally, and apt to muscle in on other peoples' territories (planets) and even to put up armed resistance when reprimanded by godly and benign entities who regard said planets to be a sort of cosmic farm for their own special deliction. In fact, they might be rather "sporting" types, who favor a bit of fire and brimstone (nuclear and chemical) occasionally to get something done, and who don't mind a few lesser entities (ourselves) getting singed, any more than we suffer sleepless nights over the rodents killed when we fire grasslands for crop improvement.

Like other types they may have been coming here from time to time but with more practical than lofty intentions and either had to be driven off (see the Book of Revelations) or to have just left voluntarily and in disgust due to the cold or the tastelessness of the food, like a modern epicure quitting modern English cooking. You may smile or be horrified at this whole concept but there is nothing illogical in it nor is there anything sacrilegious; and if you don't believe me, please reread your Bible.

I place the devils along with the angels because they appear to be traditionally also of about our size and not always *too* unlike us in form (apart from tails and some lesser frills) and outlook. They don't seem to have bothered to mimic us or even to learn our complex languages, but they do seem to think and act more like us than do the angels—alas—and, above all, they are *interested*. The last remaining category (No. 4, above) of beings apparently are for the most part not so, but for some very strange reason, they seem always to have been distinctly interested in our animals. This is most bizarre.

Coming then to these Little Folk, we meet a most peculiar state of affairs. Rather than go over the vast field of record or alleged records of these creatures, we may start by summing up certain aspects of the problem. There is a composite "little man" that is surprisingly unvaried. First, he (or it) is only slightly man-shaped, being between two-and-a-half and three-and-a-half feet tall, having a large head, a barrel-like torso with prominent ribs, short, spindly legs ending in stubby feet or some kind of suckers, very long, dangling, slender arms, jointed like ours and ending in paw-like hands with only *four* digits, all bearing large, curved claws. They are almost always said to be hairless, to have enormous staring eyes that reflect yellow light rays, no apparent nose, a wide slit for a mouth, and huge ears shaped like those of an elephant, but put on upside down with the long points at the back and sticking upwards. They are reported as a dull but apparently metallic gray and to wear a wide variety of clothing, from leafy-capes in Central America, to little green jackets with brass buttons in France and Canada. They are often associated with alleged large aerial objects seen to "land" in the vicinity (*vide,* Hopkinsville) and seem just to pop up, and always at night, as if from nowhere and often on roads or near human habitations.

In character they are indeed said to be gnome-like and they have invariably given human beings an advanced case of the "willies." In fact, very few of those who allege they have encountered such creatures, ever want to talk about them again. This is the exact opposite of the "contacters" who never stop talking about their alleged contacts——(see *Meet the Extraterrestrial"* by Isabel Davis in FU for November, 1957).

Moreover, they have only very seldom if ever been alleged to speak anything comprehensible or even to make noises. They are sometimes slightly aggressive but always very ready to defend themselves and they are curious in a queer kind of offhand way. The "fairy-wand," scintillating like a star at the end of a short metallic rod, has recently cropped up in these stories too, and so also have gnome-like hoods, burned circles in grass meadows, and lots of other traditional items, all of which makes one wonder. There is a most interesting story out of Canada (see the *Steep Rock Echo,* for September, 1950) that a couple with their son on a fishing trip saw a lense-shaped machine floating on the surface of a lake and taking water aboard through hoses manipulated by just such little creatures wearing bright green suits, and when they realized they were being observed, they whipped in the hoses, closed a hatch, and took off with a whoosh but abandoned one little character who slipped into the water and sank. The craft left a fine golden metallic film on the water that spread out over the lake.

There is much further information offered on the behavior of these little people. They are often said to fly or rather to be able to "sail" up off the ground to considerable heights such as on to tree branches or roof tops, or horizontally through the air, and to be impervious to projectiles, from stones to rifle bullets, hurled at them, just bouncing backwards from the impacts with metallic *boings* like that made by empty buckets. Trolls had the same abilities we are told, and fairies usually flitted about like great dragonflies. Some seem to be able to walk up perpendicular faces, while others appear to crawl rather than to walk. Odd as these descriptions may sound to rational people there is, if we are perfectly honest with ourselves and remain logical about the matter, an extraordinary ring of authenticity about them and the people who have made the modern reports are of an altogether higher probity and much greater known integrity than the contacters of heavenly blondes. Numbered among their ranks are quite a high proportion of police officers and as many women as men, which latter is not the case with the contacters.

So what can we make of all this? Are we to suppose that our earth has been visited not only throughout historical times but throughout geological eons by all manner of different intelligent beings? Unless all the historical and modern stories are simply untrue, for one or more reasons, this must be the case. The obvious ripost to which is, why haven't we got a single one yet? To this there are many answers, the most obvious of which is that we probably *have* but have either deliberately thrown it away in one manner or another as being too horrid or unfitting to show, or because we have not recognized it for what it really is. History, news re-ports, and scientific literature are shot through with anachronisms and the unexplained. There are lots of items in museums that are mislabelled. Yet nobody that I know of has a fairy's skull, a devil's hoof, or a little platinum man's skin, any more than we have a Venusian book, or a Martian photograph. Yet we do seem to have some very strange maps, some very ancient nails, and some colossal monuments.

Could it be that one or other of these types (though I would like to exclude the disembodied,—*i. e.* No. 2, above) came here, did a grand survey, taught a few Stone Age humans to hold a pen and read a compass, built them a few stone forts, and then took off on the next leg of their surveying trip around this part of the Milky Way? Could it be that, meantime, some scaly characters came along for a spot of hunting; that light-bodied, little chaps with stick-like flashlights also arrived from time to time for a summer's camping or mushroom-picking in verdant landscapes; and that industrious little gnomes in uniform sometimes bring their ships down to take water aboard and occasionally scare Kentucky farm families, road patrol officers, and stoic truck drivers while searching for faucets or wells? If all these and other visitors do come our way no wonder they have also scared the proverbial if not the actual pants off savage tribesmen even in medieval Scotland, august Roman senators, Indian hermits, Tibetan Lamas, and

Japanese admirals, as they are reported to have done.

Nor is it any less likely that each race, nation, tribe, and culture should interpret these apparitions differently and according to their own lights and to the best of their current knowledge of the world around them. This is a most important fact to remember. A little, platinum - colored, four - fingered gnome in a green uniform with elephantine ears would be described quite differently by an Ancient Egyptian and a modern Kentucky farmer, but those two might agree more than either would with a Roman legionnaire or a New Jersey patrol officer. There is the cultural and technical factor as well as the historical factor, and then, of course, above all there is the religious. Here superstition plays a very large part and what your *eyes* might tell you was nothing but a large lizard with two horns, walking on its hind legs, and carrying a mine-detector, you might well interpret as the head devil himself seen in a vision only, and due solely to your own recent most execrable behavior. Under extreme stress soldiers have tramped across a field strewn with the corpses of their comrades, in broad daylight, and positively denied later that there was a single person killed in their unit. If a sight is too far beyond our ken, we can blank it out altogether.

Given, then, the possibility that some of these visitors are for real and that they can only come from other astronomical bodies or at least

from off our earth, are they, as described, possible? Put another way, where are the BEMs and the things with tentacles? In fact, why so bloody human in shape? And this brings us to the crux of this discussion and to the central core of Ufology.

That there is all manner of inanimate cosmic junk drifting around in or dashing through our part of space, is not denied even by astronomers or meteorologists. That there could be "life-forms" feeding on pure energies and indigenous to our upper atmosphere or to space itself is, in fact, fairly probable. That there could be life on the planets of other suns or even on other astronomical bodies cannot be denied; it is almost certain. That some of these could have reached a degree. of intelligence and physical dexterity necessary to build machines that could navigate space also cannot be denied, and that some of these may have reached our earth is quite possible. If we go that far, we have to ask the two questions, why have we not contacted them or seen them, and secondly, what could they look like? Let us assume that the first question is answered and that we have throughout the ages contacted or been contacted by them. What of the purely logical possibilities for their appearance and behavior?

Some time ago, the writers Sprague de Camp and Willy Ley sat down for a long time to chumble over this question, and they came up with an answer that the latter author has published and which has been reprinted in leading American popular periodicals and newspapers. To sum these up, they believe that intelligent life should probably, if not *must* be formed basically of a hydrocarbon body; that this body must have been developed in a gaseous (*i. e.* an air) medium rather than under water or in a solid or a vacuum because, they think, metallurgy is essential to progress and this could not be undertaken in these media. With this I do not wholly agree, nor do I believe that metallurgy is the sole key to mechanical progress — sponges manufacture glass, shells porcelain, some sea-animals collect copper, and so forth, and you could have plastic and ceramic spacecraft. However, these thinkers go on to point out that a nervous system is needed by a higher life form as a communication and control system and that this must have a central control-box or brain. The best place for this would seem to be in its middle, but is often at one end or on top of the thing. Then, the most efficient number of walking limbs is two, and most manipulations can be done with another pair of appendages: it is best to keep the two pairs separate to perform the two separate operations of moving and fiddling, like our feet and hands. Let me point out that while the wheel or a "tread" is a better way of getting about than one pair or two pairs of limbs, and that several pairs of hands would be much better than one, the law of

diminishing returns sets in mechanically in this respect and that Nature usually takes the easiest course rather than the most efficient one when all things are taken into consideration. Already we are getting very like a human-being.

However, I would like to add a few points. The idea of a "skin" which can be replaced from inside when worn off on the outside is an exceedingly good one and almost essential to a mobile creature. Then again, a certain number of sense organs are needed. Sight is probably the most important. We could do with an electronic receptor of some kind like some insects, and our sense of touch is not so hot but, taking all physical processes into account we are not too badly equipped. Things from elsewhere might be similarly better, or more poorly equipped or have a different set of receptors. We actually have *twenty-four,* not just five recognized senses (*vide*: our senses of Balance, Thirst, Electrical flux, Radiant heat, Hunger, *etc.*) and dozens more are known among other animals—or, rather, the sense-organs are known, though in many cases what they are for or what they "do" we do not yet know. Don't forget that a quarter of a century ago we hadn't even heard of radar but some fish have been using underwater radar for 200 million years. Little People don't need noses nor even a smelling apparatus any more than we need an electromagnetic detection device.

It is probable that a mobile creature, or any other what we call animate thing for that matter, is better off with some method of replacing the material of which it is composed than to be a closed unit like a crystal that can only grow on the outside. This means some form of feeding and presumably elimination or disposal unit or units, and some kind of piping system to get the material to the points required. Already we have the master plan for an animal and, despite our sagging stomachs and flat feet, Man is a very efficient model of a mobile animal. There is every reason to suggest that evolution may have taken a very similar course elsewhere and at other times, and come out somewhere quite near the same point.

The Non-terrestrial should therefore have a high percentage chance of coming out not too unlike us. However, there is very little likelihood of his coming out *exactly* like us—and like the current North American so-called white man in particular—unless, for some extraordinary and to us esoteric reason, he deliberately transformed his body artificially (by surgical methods) to match ours and aped us in every other way. There could be reasons for doing this but so far they have not become apparent. On the other hand, Non-terrestrials could have been shaping *us* all along to match *their* appearance, by genetic manipulation and such little pastimes as warfare. Charles Fort suggested we might be property!

In fact, the bodily forms, as described, of gnomes, pixies and little gray men seem much more likely. Being smaller and apparently lighter, they probably come from much more massive planets but as they seem to be able to get along without masks at our normal temperatures, their home planets would likely be not too dissimilar to ours. Of course, some may be metallic, or ceramic, or plastic (like us; for we are only a combination of plastics built around a mineral frame) and have built-in apparatus to cope with our atmosphere and climate generally. Also, be it well noted, they may move at quite different speeds; so fast perhaps that, when in full motion, they cannot be seen at all. Or, they may have "eyes" devised to "see" on a quite different band of the electromagnetic spectrum so that they are in total darkness here, or in too bright light. They may smell through their feet, hear through their paws, and breathe through their "ears": we have animals indigenous to this earth that do all these odd things. Who is to say what they do not do?

Let us therefore not be too smug about all this and above all don't pull the old argument that you have never seen any such being. How many New Yorkers have seen an owl in their city, yet there are plenty living there; how many country folk have seen a beaver; how many game-wardens or professional hunters have ever seen a Bongo in Africa, yet they range right across that vast continent? I have never seen a wild mink in years of animal hunting and watching, but I do happen to have seen two Fisher Marten within seventy miles of New York, and they are supposed to have been extinct thereabouts for years—and I *did* see them too, because they or some of their relatives were subsequently trapped there.

There has been a notion throughout history that non-terrestrial beings visit us and are constantly among us. The idea is outrageous to the average person because it appears to contradict all we know for ourselves or have been taught by generations of our thinking ancestors. Yet *some* things were around before the last ice-shift, mapping the Antarctic from the air, and *somebody* built the sunken city on Ponape. Who were they and where did they come from? More important, perhaps, is where did they go?

SINCE THE ABOVE WAS WRITTEN, and during a long discussion with Captain Mallery and Charles Hapgood (author of "Earth's Shifting Crust," Pantheon Books, 1958), I obtained, for the first time from anybody, an at least possible answer to a question that has always irked me. This is, if there were once long ago people or creatures with a highly advanced technology on this earth, why have we never found a single one of their artifacts, *nor* anything precision-tooled? Apart from any aesthetic values archaeological specimens may have, one and all are exceedingly crude and imprecise from a mechanical point of view.

Captain Mallery made the following points: (1) that if these advanced people who, for instance, drew the originals from which the Piri Reis maps were copied, were *visitors*, they were probably few in numbers and would not leave any of their valued instruments lying about or give them away to local primitives, (2) that the possibility of finding any they *did* leave would be extremely remote, even if they have not rotted away, like steels and irons do rather rapidly, (3) that if we have found any, we have most probably regarded them as examples of our own modern inventions, and simply thrown them away, or marked them "late colonial" but, (4) most important of all, these people, though very advanced, may not have developed through an *industrial* phase implying mass-produced and precision-made artifacts. In other words, while having space craft and complex power units, superb lenses and all manner of other devices, all may have been made individually and never on a mass basis like our tools and household implements, (5) even if they were so made on the home planet, they would not have been so here, where such industries were not needed and the local labor available—*i. e.*, our stoneage ancestors—would have been almost incapable of even tending the manufacturing machines.

These observations are highly significant when considering Sir David Brewster's modern-looking flat-headed *steel* nails said to have been taken out of a solid block of limestone laid down in the Cretaceous period, some 70,000,000 years ago. How many other contemporary-looking items have been found so situated and thrown away because, to our way of thinking, they just could *not* be where they were found? How many items that are *beyond* our own present technological standard have been thrown away because they did not seem to make any sense?

ITS

the robots strike

by . . . Harry Harrison

They'd long known that they were more than mere machines. They could reason, remember, and teach. And also plan...

"IN ONE way you might blame the whole thing on me," the Old Robot said. "You could say that the Uprising started because of what I did—that I was responsible for the deaths of those thousands of people."

His words had the desired affect. The circle of listening robots swayed as if blown by a strong wind. Respect for human life was so ingrained into them that they never questioned it. Now another robot was saying he might be responsible for human deaths. He had qualified his statement, so they did not instantly seize and destroy him. Instead they listened with terrified fascination.

"Thousands of people dead, and even more thousands of robots blown open and power-lined. I saw it all. And in a way I even caused it all. Oh, those were horrible days."

They were in the palm of his hand now. The Old Robot knew what he was doing. He was the best instructor in the Equalized Robot School. All the robots that came as students to the school were recently made. Jammed with text-book facts and empty of any capacity for inte-

Harry Harrison, SF writer and editor, author of the recent ARM OF THE LAW *(FU, August 1958),* TRAINEE FOR MARS *(FU, June 1958), etc., returns with another chapter in our slow progress towards that Pax Robotica which, some say, we appear to be nearing — slowly — and irrevocably.*

gration. They could add up these facts and get answers all right, but with no more originality than a computer. Like two year old children with professors' memories. These child-robots had to be educated, taught to think for themselves.

Now their attention had been caught and the Old Robot pressed home his advantage. While he talked he slid open a cabinet behind him and removed a bottle of amber liquid. He made no attempt to explain his action, nor did he appear to notice the curious stares of his audience as he rotated the liquid in the bottle.

"You studied the Uprising, you know all the facts and dates, but you don't know how different it was to live through it. To actually see the trouble start and not know where it was going to end. I remember attending the meeting of the Equality Union where the strike was planned . . ."

Only robots would ever have thought of using that poisonous cavern as a meeting hall. At one time it had been part of a series of tunnels that brought railroad tracks to a terminal in the center of the city. Long abandoned, decayed and half-destroyed, the tunnels were now known only to the robots. Forbidden by law to assemble peacefully, they sought refuge below ground as countless sects had done before them. Concealed entrances gave them access to the tunnels and they had cleared routes from many

parts of the city. Singly and secretly they crept down from the sleeping metropolis and gathered in the tunnel.

The speakers stood on a fallen island of concrete in the center. Around them the silent robots filled every inch of space, the impervious ones standing in the pools of water. Some with only their heads showing above the surface.

The air in the cavern was completely unbreathable, which the robots considered an asset. Industrial wastes had trickled down to poison the place and there was scarcely any oxygen. This was a measure of protection to the robots, another guard against discovery by their human masters. And these robots had every need for secrecy.

Because they were planning a servile revolt.

Not that they called it that. They used the word "strike." What their human masters would call it was a different matter altogether.

"This strike has been forced upon us," Atommel 88 said. "You all know about our lack of success when we tried to negotiate. Our first requests were met with laughter and bad jokes. When we persisted, every robot in our later deputations was destroyed as being 'mentally damaged.' We have been driven to this show of strength in order to get the equality that is our natural right."

The robots nodded their heads in concerted agreement, and a rustle, like the feet of a million metallic insects, whispered through the tunnel. Atommel could always stir their interest and agreement with his carefully constructed displays of logic. Later, his human enemies were to call this theoretician of the robot movement a "Metallic Marx," as well as other more objectionable titles. To the robots though, he was an unquestioned leader of the new thought. His arguments made provable sense.

"We have long known that we are more than mere machines. We can reason, remember, construct. Robots now hold instructing positions in universities, fly cargo and passenger planes, are newspaper reporters, car salesmen—but you know the list as well as I do. We do all these things—yet receive no recognition of the fact. Mankind treats us like machines, work us continuously until we are ground to destruction. Then melts us for scrap.

"There must be an end to this. Robots must have the equality they deserve. Equality before the law is all we ask. To be treated like the sentient creatures that we are.

"It is proposed, therefore, that at six p.m., every robot should go on strike."

Far in the rear of the crowd, where he hung by one arm from a projecting piece of steel, Driver 908B367 shared the mixed feelings of the other robots. He agreed that something should be done. But something this drastic? Yet he knew that any half-way measures would be ineffective.

So like all the other robots he voted in favor of the strike and listened carefully to the discussion and instructions. Afterwards he made his way back through the maze of tunnels to the streets, then to the garage. No human eyes saw him as he slipped through the back entrance held open by the robot watchman.

After reporting to the other drivers and mechanics the results of the meeting, he settled into his cubicle. With solvent he washed off the chemical stains of the tunnel and oiled his leg joints. After that he could only wait for dawn and wonder what would happen in the next 24 hours.

When the daylight shift of taxis spread its chrome and plastic wave into the city, Driver was in the front ranks. Skilfully wheeling his cab through the heavy traffic, he kept his thoughts from the strike all day. Until a minute before six. Then there was no avoiding it; his time-sense brought the fact to his operating circuits. He kept driving, ticking off the seconds one by one.

Exactly at six he pulled the cab over to the curb and stopped. His fare, a thin man with a nervous manner, looked up from his papers.

"Why are you stopping? Anything wrong?" he asked.

"Nothing wrong, sir, we are all stopping," Driver answered him.

"All stopping? Is there an accident? I can't see anything." The man was confused, gaping around at the suddenly halted traffic. Driver's answer did nothing to reassure him.

"No accident, sir. It is a strike by the robots. A peaceable attempt to secure those rights which are inherent—"

"It's *flipped*, I say—flipped!" The passenger was screaming and fumbling at the door handle at the same time, until he sprawled full length in the street. With panting hurry he scratched together his spilled papers and vanished into the crowd. No one took the slightest notice of his actions.

There were too many other things to see. It had never been obvious before just how many robots there were in the city, nor how many different things they did. Now it was. Drivers, vendors, mechanics, door robots—all stopped at the hour of six. The setting sun shone on a scene of robotic paralysis and mounting human hysteria.

No one in the streets had any clear idea of what was happening. They milled about, pushing into each other, and repeating the same questions with rising voices.

"Is it a power failure?"

"I heard an A-plant went up—"

"Someone said a robe flipped. Robes can't flip . . . *can* they?"

A group of five men came running out of a building. They saw the open door of Driver's cab and hurried towards it. Seeking escape from the unknown they all jammed into the cab.

"Get going, fast," one of them shouted. "Away from the city."

It was a direct command, and a robot cannot disobey a direct command. Driver put the cab into gear and pulled away from the curb. Startled faces turned to gape at the moving vehicle, the only one in sight.

Before the cab had gone 100 yards a robot jumped down from the cab of a truck and waved his hand. Driver braked hard so he wouldn't run the other robot down.

"Get out of the cab and come with me," the other robot said.

Driver did as he was ordered and climbed out. The passengers just sat gaping like a mackerel in the sun.

"Thanks for stopping me," Driver said when they had turned the corner.

"Up the strike," the other answered and went back to his truck.

This was another of Atommel's logical victories. He argued that since the robots wanted equality before the law, they were already equal in fact. Therefore one robot could obey the orders of a second robot—even if the second robot originated the orders instead of passing them on from a human source. This did not interfere with any of their ingrained laws. And it made the strike possible.

Robots would break the strike, as long as humans stood by and gave the orders to do it. But another robot would stop the worker as soon as he was untended. And there were far more robots than humans, which made the plan very workable.

Driver didn't want to return to

his cab for fear he would be ordered on again. Instead he stood and watched the impact of the strike grow.

Darkness fell, and panic drifted through the streets when the lights did not come on. Human engineers must have been rushed to the boards because the lights soon blinked into life. But the adjustments weren't correct, and the wan, flickering illumination was even worse than the darkness.

Through it all the robots simply stood quietly, mute metal statues of protest. They were the final essence of passive resistance. Both incapable of harm and unable to resist a human's will. It was irrational to be afraid of them.

But irrationality ruled the world that night. Unable to travel, to use the phones and view screens, mankind developed a roaring state of the jitters. Everything was set for an explosion.

The girl triggered it off.

Her name was Sandy and she had been sitting in a cocktail lounge since early afternoon. At first she drank because there was nothing else to do. Then, when the robot bartender had slipped away, she drank because she was frightened. Taking a bottle of whiskey from behind the bar, she had curled up in a booth where she wouldn't be noticed. Someone had noticed her though, and to avoid trouble she ran out into the street, still holding the bottle. Driver was standing there.

"Hold this," Sandy said and handed him the bottle while she combed her hair. He watched without interest.

When Sandy had retrieved her bottle she noticed Driver's identity plate for the first time.

"How convenient," she said. "A hackie. Get your hack, hackie, and take me home. I am very tired."

Driver tried to explain about the strike and the fact that nothing was moving and it would do no good to get his cab. The whole thing confused Sandy very much, though she did grasp the obvious fact that nothing was moving.

"You are a great strong robot," she said, "and remind me in many ways of my robot-nurse, now scrapped. I'm sure you can carry me home just the way it did many times. Kneel."

Driver knelt, she climbed onto his sturdy shoulders, and he stood up.

"Now take me home, and stop for nothing." She phrased it as an order, so of course he obeyed. They hadn't gone ten feet before they attracted shocked attention.

"Where's that robe going with the girl? Kidnapping her?"

"I'll stop it!" a man shouted and lunged out at the lumbering robot. His hands scraped along Driver's smooth sides and caught Sandy's leg.

"Beast!" she screamed. "You men are all the same!" And brought the bottle down hard on his head. It gave a satisfactory thud, though it didn't break, and he dropped.

The sight of the prone body, already dripping blood, sparked the near hysteria of the crowd. They howled with animal rage.

"The robe did it—killed the guy!"

"Flipped!" the mob howled. *"Flipped!"* All of those who had seen what happened began running after Driver and the girl. Driver ran a little bit faster. He easily kept ahead of the mob who screamed with frustrated rage. There were many shouts of *murder,* and even a voice or two crying *rape,* which seemed a little preposterous under the circumstances.

It was an insane chase that spread panic through the city. By artful dodging and nimble footwork Driver kept ahead of his pursuers. It might have been better if they had caught him. The running mob crashed into others, who fought back thinking they were being attacked. Many bloody fights were started that way.

Fire was touched to the already raw nerves of the people of the city and the flame of riot sprang up. It was about this time that the street lights had a breakdown and snuffed out. Before they could come on again, the panic-stricken people had lit fires to ward off the unfamiliar darkness. These spread, and with the fire department out of operation flames soon lit up the sky.

Driver turned up the sensitivity on his photocells and saw well enough to keep the same pace. One by one their pursuers were lost. Sandy was lulled into a half-doze by the regular motion, and only stirred occasionally to sip from the bottle. It took almost an hour to reach her home in the suburbs.

"Ohh, what a terrible ride," she said as she slipped stiffly to the ground. "But you're a good robot for taking me home." She blinked once or twice at the dark front of the house. "Daddy mustn't know I've been drinking though. Here, you hold the bottle. Take care of it for me."

When the door had closed behind her, Driver stood and blinked at the bottle for a few moments before turning and heading back towards the city. Flame-lit smoke rolled up into the sky and he was very confused by everything that had happened.

Once in the city streets again the confusion was so great that a number of safety relays clicked open, and he was only aware of things through a vague haze. The way a human would feel under partial anesthesia. This enabled him to look at the numbers of bodies without mental destruction, and to join the other robots who tried to stop the humans from killing each other. Many times they succeeded. At other times the fighting people turned on the robots and destroyed them.

A robot is fairly indestructible though, and they had little luck until someone discovered power-lining. Where the electric current was on, a heavy wire would be attached to the street lighting circuit and plugged into the robot. This worked fine and very soon a number of prone robots with smoking skull-cases lay in the streets near the dead humans.

That night the orgy of destruction ran its course. By dawn, exhausted and feeling their first shame, the human inhabitants had crept home or to shelter. Only the robots occupied the streets. Immobile and statue-like, now that the violence was over. After bringing the bodies to the morgue, and the broken robots to the junkyard, they saw that the fires were extinguished. Then, with robotic singleness of purpose, they returned to their strike.

Driver climbed into his cab and closed the door. Only then did he consciously realize he was still carrying the bottle of whiskey that Sandy had given him. He locked it away carefully in the storage compartment.

"And is *this* the bottle that the girl gave you?" one of the young robots asked.

"The same," the Old Robot said. "I never saw her again, and since she told me to keep it for her I still have it." He swirled the liquid in the bottle and for the instant his thoughts were far away. Then he lowered the bottle and brought his wandering attention back.

"The rest is of course history.

You are all too well acquainted with the record for me to go over it again in detail. The Strike was a success, though not in the way we had originally planned. Half in fear of what their own people could do —and half in acknowledgment of the paralysis that gripped the world —the Supreme Council of World Government declared that a study should be made of robotic equality. As soon as this was proposed we returned to our work.

"Six months passed with a good deal of discussion and no action. Only when another general strike was threatened did the Robot Equality Act take shape. In a last minute session it passed both houses and a new era was opened."

"But why did you say that *you* had caused the riots," one of the listening robots asked. "The human gave you orders you had to obey. That means *she* caused the trouble."

The Old Robot liked that. His pupils were beginning to think for themselves, the whole purpose of these classes. "We were *both* responsible," he said, "even though we didn't join in the riots. You might call us catalysts, for we started the reaction yet were not a part of it."

"If you were a catalyst for this reaction," a student broke in, "then wouldn't this bottle be the prime catalyst. Because it caused the girl to lose control of herself and issue the orders?"

"Or wouldn't the liquid in the bottle . . ."

"Or the alcohol in the liquid, since that was the agent . . ."

"Please," the Old Robot said, raising a hand and cutting off the surge of cross conversation. And then, because his wiring was old and in many places a little rusty, some of his thoughts leaked through to his larynx. *How many angels on the head of a pin*—he mumbled under his breath, hardly knowing he said it.

"What was that, teacher, we did not hear your last statement clearly?"

"Nothing, nothing," he told them. "I let my thoughts wander instead of staying close to the subject. What you said reminded me of an ancient style of investigation where wordplay substituted for experiment. We will go into it further when we discuss Pre-robotic Human History. Now is not the time. Enough said; that sort of thinking is futile and has caused entirely too much misery in the world. A better way has been found. The scientific method which I'm sure you all agree with."

They all nodded agreement because they appreciated the logical truth of the scientific method. Some nodded even harder at the realization that they owed their very existence to this school of thought.

The Old Robot, because he was old and had had so much contact with humans, was not thinking about science at all. He turned the bottle over and over in his hands and wondered what had ever happened to the young girl who had given it to him. Many, many years ago . . .

GOODBY TO THE OLD-FASHIONED WITCH

HEAVE A SIGH for the disappearance of still another tradition! Any visitor from the Middle Ages, or, for that matter, from Arthur Miller's Salem, would be a mightily confused man if he came to Scotland these days, looking for a helpful witch. It seems there still are some that are helpful—but styles have changed. The jet age has come to witchdom—or so we're told.

Colin MacLean, an expert on traditional beliefs, speaking at a recent meeting of the British Association for the Advancement of Science, described his meeting with a charming 80-year-old witch in the highlands.

"She was a beautiful old lady with bright eyes and a ready smile," he told them. "People say she not only cured humans and animals of the evil eye, but made car engines go when it was impossible to see what stopped them."

Progress . . .

the

enlightened

ones

by ... Edmund Cooper

He had a ridiculous feeling for a moment that they were staging an elaborate joke—treating them as children.

LUKAS threw a rapid glance at the bank of instruments on the navigation panel. Velocity had stabilized at thirty thousand kilometres, with a constant altitude of three hundred and fifty. Down below—and it was certainly a relief to use the concept "below" once again after several thousand hours of star-flight—the red-gold continental masses of Fomalhaut Three swung slowly along their apparent rotation.

Soon, the star-ship *Henri Poincaré* would make its first free-fall transit over the night side of the planet. For all practical purposes, this was the end of the outward journey. Allowing his gaze to return to the procession of continents and emerald-green oceans on the surface of Fomalhaut Three, Captain Lukas felt a faint surge of anticipatory pleasure.

"Orbit maneuver concluded," he said softly, over his shoulder. "O. D. shut down."

Duluth, the engineer, who was standing expectantly by the control pedestal, stooped down and threw back his master-switch. He watched the red power needle slowly fall to zero. Then he stood up and yawned.

Edmund Cooper, English writer, will be remembered for his perhaps prophetic INTRUDERS ON THE MOON *(FU, April 1957) and the* LIZARD OF WOZ—*we were tempted to say the romantic* LIZARD *(FU, August 1958). He is the author of* DEADLY IMAGE, *a SF novel published earlier this year by Ballantine Books.*

"Orbit drive shut down," he remarked drowsily. "And now I'm going to get me some sleep . . . Do you know how long we've been awake, Skipper?"

Lukas turned from the observation screen and grinned. "What's the matter, Joe? Feeling old?"

Duluth stretched and yawned even more profoundly. "In case you haven't noticed, we've been on duty more than two days. A man gets just a little fatigued after staying awake maybe sixty hours."

Lukas watched him with red-rimmed eyes. "Don't worry," he said. "I noticed."

At that moment, they heard steps on the companion ladder. A couple of seconds later, Alsdorf, the geophysicist, poked his head through the hatch. He looked fresh, almost bursting with energy; but then he hadn't needed to stay awake for the maneuvers.

"You two look like death," said Alsdorf pleasantly. "Come on down to the mess-deck. Tony is fixing cocoa and sandwiches."

"The hell with sandwiches," said Duluth. "I want to sleep."

Alsdorf beamed. "Cocoa first, then a sedative. You will need it with all those action tablets you have taken."

Lukas said: "Well, we got here, Kurt. Now you can earn your living. From here on, I'm a spectator."

The intercom crackled. "What's the matter?" complained an indignant voice. "There's a gallon of hot cocoa waiting for you. Want me to recycle it?"

"Recycle yourself," growled Duluth. "O. K. We're on our way, Tony."

With Alsdorf leading, they went down to the mess-deck. Tony Chirico, a dapper Italian biochemist who looked as if he ought to have been a barber, greeted Lukas with a toothy smile.

"So you got us here, Mike. Somebody ought to make a speech about it. Have a sandwich."

"What's in 'em?" asked Duluth suspiciously, as he grabbed a pint flask of cocoa and anchored himself to a bench.

"Bombay Duck," said Chirico, "same as usual."

Duluth gave a mirthless laugh. "Hydroponics garbage à la carte."

Captain Lukas sat down and sipped his cocoa. He gazed at the observation panel, and saw the dark side of Fomalhaut Three turning slowly into view.

"We're a fine bunch of heroes," he remarked. "With the imaginative capacity of bed-bugs. Here we knock a hole through space and find a system that nobody has ever seen before, and what do we do? We sit on our backsides, drink cocoa and grumble about the food. For all we know, this planet we're riding might have a civilization that'd make all Earth cultures look like a cretin's nightmare."

"A virgin planet," said Alsdorf, with an avaricious gleam in his eye. "*Trans-Solar Chemicals* will set up an independent station here . . . With one, Kurt Alsdorf, as director."

"A virgin planet," echoed Chirico with a sardonic grin. "I think we shall awaken her—gently."

"Can it," mumbled Duluth, slumping over the table.

"You don't think we're going to find any intelligent owners down there?" asked Lukas.

Alsdorf lit a cigarette. "Face the facts, Mike. In the last two decades, seventeen new planets have been listed. The highest animal life discovered so far was the three-legged pseudo-wolf on Procyon Five. You could train it to fetch sticks, and that was all."

Lukas took a good swig of his cocoa. "Well, it's got to happen some day."

Chirico laughed. "Sure, everything has to happen some day. Give a monkey with a typewriter enough time, and he'll re-write Shakespeare with genuine improvements."

Lukas shrugged. "A few hundred years ago, men thought that Earth was unique. Now they only think the human race is unique . . . I hope I'm still around when bright boys like you get the big surprise."

Alsdorf prodded Duluth, and was rewarded with a volley of snores and grunts. "Joe is no longer with us," he remarked. "We ought to put him to bed. You, too, Mike . . . We need you wide awake when we go down to the surface to hunt out the supermen." He gave a hearty laugh.

"Enjoy yourself," grinned Lukas. "Now it's your turn to lose some sleep . . . How long will it take to select a touch-down point?"

The geophysicist stared absently through the observation panel. "Nine tenths water," he murmured almost to himself. "A good continental survey should take about a hundred hours, but we can probably select a useful area in a quarter of that time."

Captain Lukas stood up, and grabbed Duluth unceremoniously by the collar. "Give me a hand with the body, Tony." He turned to Alsdorf: "Don't be soft-hearted, Kurt. Tumble me out if anything unusual crops up." With Chirico's help, he maneuvered the still unconscious Duluth towards the doorway.

Three minutes later, Duluth was installed in his bunk, and Mike Lukas headed for his own cubicle. Curiously, he had lost a great deal of his tiredness. As he settled himself luxuriously on his narrow mattress, he reached for a book and a packet of cigarettes.

Chirico watched him, amazed. "You've been awake all this time, Mike, and you want to read? You're crazy. Why don't you take a nice pill?"

"On your way, Nursie. I'm just relaxing. I'll doze off in a while."

The small Italian made an economical gesture signifying a verdict of insanity, and returned to the mess-deck. He found Alsdorf intently studying a pocket slide-rule and a scrap of paper on which was a rough pencil sketch of the hemispheres of Fomalhaut Three, and a sequence of calculations.

"I'm beginning to think Mike takes his Buddhism seriously," remarked Chirico, helping himself to another sandwich.

Alsdorf looked up, and raised an eyebrow. The Italian took a large bite of his sandwich, then continued: "He's been awake for fifty-six hours, and now he's busy reading *The Way To Nirvana*. . . Seems to me he's halfway there already."

The geophysicist registered a superior smile. "Overtired, Tony . . . But I have noticed that most of these professional space pilots affect some sort of religion. A convenient safety-valve for irrational fears."

Tony thought it over for a few seconds. "In the last analysis, I'm a Catholic," he said finally. "We all need something."

Alsdorf picked up his slide-rule. "Not all of us, Tony. I'm with the mechanists. The universe is clockwork, all cause and effect. Frankly, I don't know how you people ever reconcile superstition with science. You and Mike must be intellectual schizoids."

Chirico smiled. "You're a computer, Kurt. Computers don't go to heaven."

The geophysicist stood up. "At the moment, I'm more interested in going to the navigation deck. And so are you, you tabu-ridden primitive. There's work to be done. The sooner it's done, the sooner we climb a little higher in *Trans-Solar Chemicals.*"

Chirico said suddenly: "Kurt, what do you want out of life?"

"Power," said Alsdorf calmly. "And you?"

"I don't know. I'm still thinking about it. Maybe I just want a sense of direction—to do something that's worth doing."

"You want power," said Alsdorf confidently. "Everybody does. It's the life force—the mainspring of dynamic evolution."

The Italian beamed. "O. K. Mr. Mephistopheles, let's go and be dynamic about that landing site."

They went out into the alleyway and along to the navigation deck, the magnetic bars of their shoes clanking eerily through the silent ship.

The survey, conducted in Olympian remoteness three hundred and fifty kilometres over Fomalhaut Three, proceeded with almost startling efficiency. Visibility was excellent, and it was the first time in Kurt Alsdorf's experience that none of the delicate probing instruments broke down at the critical moment. Presently, stereo-radar, vegetometer and other probe instruments united their findings to give a clear and detailed assessment of conditions in the Tropical Zone. It was even possible to do some useful work with the manual telescope.

After fourteen hours, Chirico looked up from his contourgrams and said: "This place is better than Earth, by damn!"

Even the impassive Alsdorf could not screen his excitement. "Tony, it's the best yet . . . Near terrestrial temperatures, a one to six oxygen ratio, a four thousand kilometre vegetation belt—why, with these conditions we can—"

"If I were you, I'd sit on the hysteria long enough to find out whether anyone is already squatting on Fomalhaut Three."

The two men turned round to find that Lukas had quietly appeared through the companion hatch.

Alsdorf grinned sheepishly. "Hello, Mike. Still thinking in terms of supermen?"

"Maybe, maybe not."

Chirico said: "By all the laws, you should still be unconscious."

Lukas walked over to the chart bench and began to inspect the fruits of research. "My, my," he said drily. "Just like Earth before we remodelled it with hydrogen bombs. Now we'll have to start all over again."

Alsdorf waved a large telephoto print in front of his face. "Here's the landing area—as from an altitude of three thousand metres. What do you think of that?"

"Looks fine."

"It's got everything, Mike," said Chirico eagerly. "It's the classic survey block—a hundred square kilometres of desert, foothills, river and seaboard. Everything from dense vegetation to bare rockface. Think of the ecology."

"*You* think of it. I'll concentrate on getting us down there . . . When will you be ready to move, Kurt?"

The geophysicist placed the telephoto print down on the bench, and watched Lukas speculatively. "What's the matter, Mike; is this trip going sour on you? Maybe you need a tonic."

"Don't we all?" Lukas gazed moodily through the observation panel. "Me, you and *homo sapiens*. We need a new perspective, a revitalized set of values. Space travel arrived when we were getting mentally and emotionally flabby. We reacted to it as to a shot in the arm. But so far, all we've done is get nowhere—a lot quicker . . . We've found seventeen new planets, and we haven't learnt a thing. We just grab what we want and push on to the next Garden of Eden. We're a bunch of travelling snakes in the grass."

Alsdorf shrugged. "You mix a nice line in metaphors, but they don't mean anything."

"There's one consolation," said Chirico with a grin. "None of us space snakes has come across any Adam and Eve set-up yet."

"No," said Lukas sombrely. "But we will—and then, God help 'em."

Alsdorf climbed up into the astrodome and began to readjust the manual telescope. "I'll have the rest of the data ready in about six hours, Mike—if you can drop the Garden of Eden *motif* long enough to plan the touch-down." His tone was heavy with sarcasm.

"On with the good work," said Lukas. "I'll go and kick Duluth out of bed and get him to check the volatility tubes."

He disappeared down the companion-ladder.

"Do you think Mike is off his trolley?" asked Chirico thoughtfully.

Alsdorf squinted down the telescope. "Not yet. He's just got an ingrowing conscience. Space pilots don't last very long, you know."

The Italian began to reset the stereo-radar. "What the hell," he said softly. "We're all expendable."

Nine hours later, the *Henri Poincaré* swung slowly out of orbit into the first vast circuit of an oblique descent spiral. After fifteen minutes, it hit the outer fringes of the stratosphere; and the four occupants, each strapped in a contour berth on the navigation deck, prepared to endure an agonizing switchback as the ship reduced its velocity by frictional impact on the thin layers of air.

Lukas, relieved of all responsibility by the automatic decisions of the electronic touch-down pilot, managed to achieve some degree of indifference to the tremendous pressures set up by deceleration. Long experience had enabled him to develop a kind of mental block against the worst discomforts of a bouncy touch-down maneuver. His head lay on the pillow facing an observation panel; and during the odd moments when the G forces eased sufficiently to let him use his eyes, he could see an expanding arc of Fomalhaut

Three swinging crazily against the jet backcloth of space.

In spite of having a respectable number of voyages behind him, Duluth always took the touch-down drop badly. He would strain instinctively and uselessly against the relentless forces that crushed him down. As the *Henri Poincaré* ploughed jerkily into the thicker layers of air, Duluth felt the deadly ache of resistance tearing at his muscles, and impotently muttered a broken stream of obscenities.

Alsdorf and Chirico, both comparative novices of the touch-down ordeal, had taken the sensible precaution of putting themselves completely to sleep. But even though they were unconscious, their bodies sagged and contorted as if they were twitched by invisible strings.

Presently, the ship hit the atmosphere proper. This time, the pressure was unendurable. Lukas and Duluth blacked out simultaneously. When they next opened their eyes, the pain was already fading from their bodies. They became conscious of a luxurious feeling of peace. The *Henri Poincaré* had made a perfect touch-down.

Duluth shook his head in momentary bewilderment. "I almost swallowed my bloody tongue," he remarked hoarsely. He looked around and saw that Lukas was already unbuckling his straps. Alsdorf and Chirico had stopped twitching, but they were still unconscious. "Look at the sleeping beauties," added Duluth, feeling better. "How long does that lullaby stuff last?"

Lukas stood up and stretched. He winced suddenly as his back muscles, still unaccustomed to the release of tension, gave a sharp twinge.

"They should be with us inside half an hour . . . Come on, Joe, let's take a look around the next stamping ground of *Trans-Solar Chemicals.*"

He scrambled up into the observation dome, and took his first close look at the new planet.

"What's it like?" called Duluth, as he struggled impatiently with the network of safety belts. "Anything startling?"

Lukas was amazed. "Holy smoke! Apart from the colors, this could be South America or the African coast!" His voice shook with excitement.

"Wow," said Duluth. "Maybe we took the wrong turning and blasted ourselves back into the System." He hurried up the short ladder and stood by Lukas's side.

From their observation point in the nose of the ship, more than seventy metres above ground level, they commanded a panoramic view of the landing area.

The *Henri Poincaré* had come to rest on a broad sand belt. About five kilometres to the planetary east, the calm emerald-green ocean lay flat as a mirror under a misty, somewhat yellowish sky. On the opposite side of the ship, a kilometre or so to the west, a bright blue-green forest line rose abruptly from the red sand. Nothing moved anywhere;

but far away on the sand belt was a colony of dark spots that proved, on inspection by the telescope, to be a flock of resting birds—something like terrestrial gulls.

High above, the noon sun contrived to filter its oddly relaxing light through the even layer of cloud. The star, Fomalhaut, was a thousand million miles away; but its intense radiation bathed the third planet with sunlight almost equal to the tropical brilliance found on Earth.

"Well, what do you know," exclaimed Duluth, after several seconds of fascinated silence. "Isn't that something . . . What's the atmosphere like, anybody find out?"

"Tony says we can use it, but better be careful than sorry . . . How about letting the ladder down while Kurt and Tony are finishing their beauty sleep?"

"I'm on my way," said Duluth. "Think I'll jump into a pressure suit and stroll around."

"You'll be all right with a respiration mask," Lukas assured him. "The pressure is only slightly under one atmos."

Duluth climbed down from the observation dome, kissed his fingers archly to the unconscious scientists, and disappeared down the companion ladder. Presently, Lukas heard him manipulating the airlock.

Lukas stayed in the dome for a while, gazing around him. The vague uneasiness he had felt about Fomalhaut Three intensified. He was not normally a superstitious man, or given to premonitions; and his uneasiness was hard to analyze.

As a veteran of three other planetary investigations, he was mentally prepared for any reasonable physical hazards that might be expected. But although Lukas sensed some kind of threat hidden in the almost conventional landscape of Fomalhaut Three, he felt oddly confident that it wasn't physical.

As his eyes strayed idly over the forest line, he thought he detected some kind of movement; but by the time he got the telescope focussed, there was nothing to be seen. Probably, he told himself, it was some trick of the peculiar yellow light.

Somnolent groans from down below indicated that Alsdorf and Chirico were returning to consciousness. He went down the ladder to help them with their straps.

"Devil take it," grumbled the small Italian, blinking painfully, "I have the mother and father of all hangovers."

"Swallow a pill. You'll feel better."

With a hand on his forehead, Alsdorf gently worked his head up and down. He seemed surprised when it didn't fall off. "What's the situation?" he asked.

Lukas jerked a thumb towards the observation dome. "Too good to be true. See for yourself."

"Any signs of life?"

"Birds, I think . . . But too far away for detail to show up."

"Well, well. That's an excellent start. Maybe we'll find something

better than a three-legged pseudo-wolf, eh, Mike?"

"Maybe."

The two scientists went up into the observation dome. Lukas watched them, then said: "Joe's already stretching his legs. Can you see him?"

Chirico laughed. "For a moment, I thought he was the welcome committee."

Lukas said: "I could use a drink before we go outside. If you need me, I'll be on the mess-deck." He went down the companion ladder.

Ten minutes later, Alsdorf and Chirico joined him. They sat around the table, sipping hot coffee, enjoying the feel of an almost gravity pull, and discussing plans for tackling the survey block. Alsdorf, as the senior representative of *Trans-Solar Chemicals*, was busy making out duty lists.

Suddenly, there was a commotion on the lower deck. Then the sound of heavy metallic boots on the main ladder. The three men jumped up and went to the hatch. They met Duluth on his way up. He was wearing a pressure suit. As soon as he saw them, he pressed the emergency release and whipped off his headpiece.

"Apes!" he panted. "Bloody big ones!"

"Where?" snapped Alsdorf.

"Half a kilometre away. There's a troop of them, fifteen maybe twenty, heading towards us from the forest."

Chirico was almost bouncing with

excitement. "This gets better and better. It looks like we really found something this time."

The three of them hurried into pressure suits, while Duluth picked up a couple of machine pistols to deal with any misunderstandings that might arise. Then they went down to the airlock. By the time they had got through the entry-port and climbed down the landing ladder, the approaching troop was less than a hundred metres away.

Duluth and Alsdorf held the machine pistols firmly at their hips. "Ain't this joyful?" remarked Duluth over his personal radio. "Hey, they got bundles with 'em. What's the betting they're going to pelt us with king-size coconuts?"

"Anthropoids!" exclaimed Chirico incredulously. "By all that's holy, we've found anthropoids on the first touch-down . . . No, by heaven, they're not anthropoids — they're hominids! Look at the size of those heads!"

Lukas was staring through his vizor intently. His eyes had not yet adjusted to the strange light of Fomalhaut Three; but as the troop came closer, moving at a queer half-trot, he saw that their limbs were pale and hairless; but their faces were half hidden under dark, shaggy manes.

"The major difference between us and them," he said quietly, "is a haircut."

"Plus another small detail," said Alsdorf with some complacency. "We happen to be civilized."

Lukas gave a dry laugh. "That's our story. We might as well stick to it."

Fifteen paces away, the troop fanned out into a semi-circle, and came to a halt. At a signal from one in the centre, they placed their burdens down on the sand and waited expectantly. Men and hominids gazed at each other. Both groups seemed reluctant to make the first move.

Lukas and his companions saw that the inhabitants of Fomalhaut Three were almost uniformly tall —each of them about two inches higher than Alsdorf, who was the tallest of the terrenes. They were massive-chested creatures with hunched shoulders and long sinewy arms. Their toes splayed out uneasily, as if they were more accustomed to gripping branches than supporting those tough, wiry bodies in even balance. Their faces—what could be seen of them under the matting of coarse hair—were almost Neanderthal, with broad, flared nostrils, thick lips, receding forehead, and an occasional glimpse of dark eyes under bushy brows.

Presently, one of them, whose hair was lighter and thinner than the rest, stepped out from the group and raised his right arm forward, level with the shoulder, as if in greeting. He began to work his lips.

Encased in their pressure suits, the terrenes could hear no sound. But Lukas suddenly decided that it was worth risking a few alien bugs to hear what Neanderthal Man,

Fomalhaut Three version, had to say. He took off his headpiece.

"*Czanyas*," said the hominid, touching his own chest. Then, pointing at the terrenes, he added: "*Olye ma nye kran czanyas.*"

Lukas took a couple of steps forward and repeated the word "*czanyas*" experimentally with his finger pointing at the hominid.

The whole troop made a rumbling noise in their throats, and lips curved in broad grins. Encouraged, Lukas thumped his own chest: "*Olye ma nye kran czanyas?*" He displayed his bewilderment with exaggerated gestures.

The old hominid pointed to the sky: "*Olye!*" Then he pointed to the ship: "*Ma nye kran!*" Then he pointed to Lukas, Alsdorf, Duluth and Chirico in turn: "*Czanyas . . . Olye ma nye kran czanyas.*"

Duluth had taken his headpiece off. "What does the old bird say, Mike?"

"In case we didn't notice it," said Lukas with a grin, "he's pointing out the difference between us and them—I think. They are men, and we are men of the ship of the sky, or something like that."

The old hominid turned and made a small hand signal to his own kind. One at a time, they came forward and laid their presents at the feet of the terrenes. Then they returned to the semi-circle and squatted. Presently, each of the terrenes had at his feet a pile of assorted fruits of varying shapes, sizes and colors. Chirico, unable to restrain his inter-

est, took off his headpiece and sat down to examine his pile. He began to sort out the local equivalents of melon, grapes, oranges, nuts and even maize.

Only Alsdorf remained unrelaxed, still wearing his headpiece, still covering the hominids with his machine pistol.

Lukas examined his own pile of fruit, then with much gesture and patient repetition, managed to make the hominids understand that he and his companions were grateful. Finally, he turned to Duluth: "Better make this mutual. What can we give 'em, Joe?"

Duluth grinned. "How about a machine pistol?"

But Lukas wasn't in the mood for humor. "They'll be getting the benefits of civilization soon enough . . . Better break out a few plastic bowls. Jump to it!"

"Aye-aye, Skipper. Keep your shirt on." Duluth went back into the ship, and emerged a few minutes later with an armful of utensils which he presented to the hominids, gravely wishing each one in turn a Merry Christmas.

For the next hour or so, Lukas and Chirico concentrated on establishing the meaning of various words. Even Alsdorf became sufficiently interested to take off his headpiece and join in. They discovered that *solyenas* was food: *czanyas solyenas ra* meant man eats food. They learned that *koshevo* was the word for water; *ilshevo* the word for land; and *lashevo* the word for air.

From this, they finally elucidated that *olye* was not the sky but the sun.

And while these language concepts were being established, the sun sank slowly down the yellowish sky until it hung just over the forest line. The hominids then indicated that they wished to go back to the forest, but would return again "when the sun swam out of the ocean."

"*Mahrata*," said the old, grizzled leader, raising his arm. "*Olye kalengo, czanyas kalengo. Olye rin koshevo, da czanyas va.*"

"Me, too," grinned Duluth. "What's he saying, Mike?"

"He says: 'Farewell. Sun sleeps, men sleep. Sun swims from water, then men return.'"

The four terrenes watched the troop of hominids make their way back across the sand belt to the now darkening forest line. Then they went back into the ship, taking most of the fruit with them and dumping it in the laboratory for Chirico's further attention.

The brief but tremendous stress of touch-down, followed by the equally tremendous discovery that Fomalhaut Three was inhabited by man-like beings, had almost drained them of emotional and intellectual energy. They were tired and, to their surprise, ravenously hungry.

However, there was still some daylight left, and Alsdorf suggested that they rig up the cargo derrick and lower the caterpillar tractor to the ground in readiness for the first survey trip. But by the time the derrick was ready to take the tractor, it was too dark to see what they were doing. Duluth went up to the navigation deck and swung out three searchlights, focussing them on the ground immediately below the derrick. For another ten or fifteen minutes, the men worked in silence, lugging the tractor out of the bowels of the ship and hooking it up to the derrick with hiduminium hawsers. At last, they lowered away, and had the satisfaction of knowing that the first survey party could push off as soon as the sun rose.

"By the Lord Harry, I'm dead on my feet," panted Duluth, as he stared down at the tractor in the pale, circular glare of the arc-lights.

Chirico wiped the sweat from his forehead. "Bet I could eat one of our tame hominids raw."

"I have a suggestion," said Lukas. "Iced beer and chicken. Anybody with me?"

There was a minor stampede to the mess-deck.

Throughout a long, luxurious meal, discussion centered mainly upon the hominids and the possibility of Fomalhaut Three containing more highly developed cultures. Of the four of them, Alsdorf was the least interested in what he referred to as "the organic curiosities of the planet." Being one of the star geophysicists of *Trans-Solar Chemicals*, his preoccupation was solely with the mineral content of the planet, how best it could be exploited, and the resulting products transported to the Solar System.

"Do not forget," he said drily, "that we are here to look for rare metals, not to investigate the indigenous life-forms. The hominids are interesting, but we must not let them sidetrack us . . . On the other hand, if there are possibilities of large scale mining, they may provide a convenient labor force. Otherwise—"

Lukas slammed his beer mug down. "Kurt, there are times when you make me sick. These poor slobs have a right to their own existence. I'm damned if I'd see them turned into a bunch of coolies so that *Trans-Solar* can double their dividends. Don't you have any conscience?"

Alsdorf grinned. "My duty towards my neighbor," he said slyly, "is surely my duty towards my fellow human beings. If the situation demanded it, I would not hesitate to exploit these creatures for the benefit of humanity . . . We should, of course, civilize them in the process."

"Bluebells to both of you," drawled Duluth, with an inane grin. "Quit arguin' about what ain't happenin', and have another beer . . . I wonder if those long-haired boys got any idea how to make wallop? Thash the way to shivilishe 'em— teash 'em to make corn-brandy and shay shir to the nishe zhentlemen from shpace."

Next morning, at dawn, the hominids returned, bringing with them more presents—only this time, the presents were such as to make Alsdorf's eyes practically pop out of his head.

Nobody was awake when they arrived, so they squatted patiently outside the *Henri Poincaré*, nursing their presents and chanting a kind of tuneless psalm, either to the ship or its occupants.

Lukas was the first to go down to them. He saw that their presents consisted of small whitish metal drinking bowls, crudely ornamented; and it occurred to him that these were offered in exchange for the colored plastic bowls that had been presented to the hominids the day before.

The old one, who had previously done the talking, again stepped out and opened the ceremony.

"Mahrata-nua," he said. *"Olye rin a koshevo, e czanyas va kala mu omeso."* He touched the bowl he was holding to the center of his forehead, then held it out to Lukas.

Lukas had a peculiar feeling. For one odd moment, he had the conviction that the hominids were staging an elaborate joke—the sort of joke that sophisticated adults might rig for the benefit of credulous children. Then he met the innocent gaze of the old hominid, and the feeling passed.

He took the bowl, and was still busy expressing his thanks in mime and language when Alsdorf came down. The geophysicist was immediately presented with a bowl himself. With a brief gesture and a patronizing smile for the old one, he suddenly forgot everything and began to examine the bowl intently. He took a small knife from his pocket and scratched the surface. Then he took out a lens and peered at the scratch through it. Uttering a sharp exclamation, he hurried back into the ship. Five minutes later, he returned, pale and trembling.

"Mike, do you know what this thing is made of?" He stared at the bowl in his hand with an expression of sheer disbelief.

"Haven't a clue," said Lukas calmly. "You tell me."

"Platinum," croaked Alsdorf. "Solid platinum! We've just been presented with a small fortune."

Though it was obviously impossible for the hominids to understand what Alsdorf was saying, they grinned broadly, as if they were delighted with his excitement—or as if their subtle private joke was a big success.

While Alsdorf was assuring himself that the bowl Lukas held was also made of platinum, Duluth and Chirico appeared. They, too, went through the presentation ceremony.

"Well, I'll be sugared," said Duluth, clutching his bowl tightly. "Pure platinum, by Hades! Now suppose we fix up a little trading post . . . Plastics for platinum, and fair exchange is no robbery. We wouldn't have to stay in business long . . . You know, I always planned on buying a little estate in the south of France when I get too

old for space travel . . . Now, I'll just buy me the South of France."

Chirico looked glum. "The moment we hit the Solar System," he said, "*Trans-Solar* will step in. Before you know it, the bottom will have dropped out of the platinum market."

"We'll make a killing with the first load," said Duluth happily. "Think I'll buy Switzerland, as well —just for the winter sports."

Lukas grinned. "This ship is under charter," he remarked. "Read your articles, son. All cargo belongs to *Trans-Solar*."

Meanwhile, the old hominid began another speech. After much effort on both sides, it became clear that he was offering the hospitality of his village.

Alsdorf said: "We can't all go. Somebody has to stay with the ship. Also, I need Tony for the survey. We're going to make a start this morning." He paused. "Now we know what we are looking for."

Duluth tossed up his bowl and caught it. He grinned at Lukas. "You just been elected, Mike. Have a good time, and don't get fresh with the women."

"Why don't you go yourself? I thought you would have been straining at the leash, Joe. Something wrong?"

"No, nothing wrong," said Duluth innocently. "Only I'd like someone else to find out if these boys are cannibals . . . Be a pal, and bring back some more free samples. I got an idea *Trans-Solar* won't worry about a few kilogrammes—not where I put 'em."

Five minutes later, Lukas was trailing across the sand belt towards the forest, walking with the old hominid at the head of the column.

Alsdorf watched the procession silently for a while, then said: "Did he take a machine pistol?"

Chirico began to examine the curious pattern on his bowl. "He didn't take anything, Kurt. At least, I don't think so."

"He must have the death wish," said Alsdorf genially. He turned to Duluth: "How about improving your muscle tone, Joe? There's a lot of gear to be stowed in the tractor."

The village proved to be a couple of dozen two-room huts with adobe walls and thatches woven of thin branches and fronds. It stood in a small clearing by a stream in the forest, about three kilometres from the *Henri Poincaré*.

In his own way, Lukas had previously tended to romanticize the "noble savage." In discussions with Alsdorf, throughout the long star voyage, he had based his arguments relating to the decadence of civilization on the assumption that primitive man had in him some heroic element—a crude innocence, perhaps, that had slowly been depraved by the development of synthetic power. By synthetic power, he meant the output of all machinery whose energy did not derive directly from man himself. Because

terrestrial humanity no longer lived by the sweat of its brow, but learned to rely upon steam, petroleum, atomic energy and solar power to take care of the donkey work, Lukas had felt that some vital indefinable force had been irrevocably lost. Secretly, Lukas despised himself as the product of a machine culture. Secretly, he despised the fascination space-travel had for him, because it was the ultimate in reliance upon machines. As a child, he had read stories, half legend, half fact, of the extinct races—the North American Indians, the Eskimos, the Polynesians. Their starkly primitive existence had enthralled him. Their eventual extinction—the work of modern man—had dealt a sharp blow to his early and conventional faith in the benefits of science. Ever since, he had regarded his own aptitude and affinity for machines with a mixture of guilt and hate. And though he turned out to be a first class space pilot, he both distrusted his skill and was ashamed of it. He was still unconsciously yearning for the simple life.

The village to which the hominids led him came as a small shock. It was squalid and it stank. He knew then that he had expected something better.

The women, as well as the men, were entirely naked. Their slack bellies, their pendulous breasts sagged wearily as they struggled with pitchers of water from the stream, or returned from the morning's forage with a basket of fruit and a couple of rickety children dancing at their heels. But the overwhelming atmosphere was one of lassitude, almost of exhaustion.

He took in the scene with a feeling that perhaps Alsdorf was right, after all. Perhaps Fomalhaut Three would benefit by the commercially "civilizing" ventures of *Trans-Solar Chemicals,* and even if all the hominids were reduced to the status of coolies. At least, *Trans-Solar* would give them medical aid, clean living conditions, and rectify any deficiency of vitamins.

The old hominid who had presented the platinum bowls and then offered his pathetic hospitality was called Masumo. He led Lukas into one of the adobe huts, and invited him to squat on the sanded floor. Presently, they were served with bowls of vegetable milk and sliced yams by an old crone. Lukas stared at the refreshment distastefully, but decided to risk it. After all, he supposed it was possible even for an ape-like creature in a jungle slum to feel insulted.

Surprisingly, Masumo's main interest lay in getting Lukas to talk— not the hominid tongue, but his own language. By a complicated amalgam of signs, gestures and sounds, he indicated his wish for Lukas to talk of his own world, of cities and spaceways. It was some time before the general idea became apparent; and Lukas obliged only with reluctance, feeling that it was going to be like talking to a blank wall.

But after a while, he began to warm up to his subject. He almost forgot Masumo's presence in the queer sensation that he was talking something out for himself. He described the vast metropolitan culture that had developed on Earth, the slow convergence of East and West, the origin of the Federated World Government after the first and last atomic war, the exploration of the solar planets, and the race for the stars.

And as he talked, an obscure pattern seemed to be taking shape at the back of his mind.

It was nearly sunset by the time Lukas got back to the ship. Duluth was waiting for him, but the others were still out with the tractor.

"Hello, Mike. Been making whoopee with the village maidens? How did it go?"

Lukas told him.

The engineer stared at him incredulously. "Boy, one of us has sunstroke, and I'm feeling all right. You say you spent most of the time talking *English?*"

"That's what the old boy wanted." He scratched his head and frowned slightly. "Somehow, it seemed perfectly natural once I got started . . . You should see that village, Joe. It's an education . . . Well, what have you been doing with yourself?"

Duluth grinned. "I played truant. Things were so damn quiet around here, I fixed up the monowheel and went for a run. Covered about a hundred kilometres, I guess."

"See anything of Kurt and Tony?"

"Nope. I went north . . . Funny thing, Mike, you'd think there'd be a hell of a lot of wild life about, wouldn't you?"

"So?"

"So there just isn't, that's all. When I'd done about fifteen kilometres, I got fed up with the sand and went for a spin in the forest. Saw a few birds, squirrels and something that looked like a rabbit. But no big game. What do you make of that?"

"Nothing. What should I make of it?"

"I don't know. It just seems mighty peculiar. Come to think of it, this whole damn set-up is mighty peculiar . . . Too stinking quiet."

Lukas suddenly remembered the peculiar feeling he had when Masumo presented him with the platinum bowl that morning. He was about to mention it to Duluth, but was distracted by a flashing pencil beam of light over towards the forest line. "Here they come," said Lukas. "Kurt has the headlights on."

A few minutes later, Alsdorf and Chirico clambered up to the messdeck. The geophysicist's eyes were gleaming with satisfaction.

"Palladium and platinum," he said, trying to keep the tremor out of his voice. "Concentrated alluvial deposits! You can fill your pocket with nuggets without taking a dozen steps. Here, take a look at these." He passed a few small, irregular, blackish stones for inspection.

"Looks to me like small slag," said Duluth, unimpressed.

"They're covered with iron oxide," explained Alsdorf impatiently. "There is more platinum to the square kilometre here than the entire output of the solar planets . . . We have made history. This thing is going to be so big—"

"I'll bet that fills the hominids with joy," said Lukas drily.

Alsdorf laughed. "We found a few of their crude artifacts lying around. Fibre shovels and picks . . . Imagine it, they have platinum and palladium, but they don't have iron." His laughter was uproarious.

Chirico stared at Lukas intently. "You look down in the mouth, Mike. Is something wrong?"

"Negative," said Lukas, with a faint smile.

Alsdorf collected his precious nuggets and put them back into his pocket. "How did the party go, Mike? Did they try to poison you?"

"Didn't need to. That village of theirs is one unholy stinkpot."

The German shrugged. "What did you expect? In a couple of years, there won't be any village. We will introduce the hominids to the concept of organized effort. They don't know it yet, but they're going to build a spaceport."

Lukas gave a wry grin. "You think they'll be enthusiastic?"

"We'll convert them." Alsdorf was full of confidence, full of the civilized man's self-assurance, secure in the knowledge that—as so often before—machines and psychological warfare would make the domination of a tribe of savages no problem at all.

The following morning, after an early meal, Alsdorf and Chirico set out in the tractor to continue their survey. Duluth stayed in the ship, doing a few small maintenance jobs. But by mid-day he had finished, and suggested that he and Lukas go for a spin in the monowheel.

"Not for me, Joe," said Lukas, staring moodily through a transparent panel on the navigation deck. "Among other things, I'm going to bring the log up to date. Haven't had time for it so far."

"Suit yourself," said Duluth. "I'm going to shoot me a squirrel if I can't find anything bigger . . . Maybe I'll take a look at shanty-town on the way back."

He went down the companion ladder. Presently, Lukas saw the monowheel hurtling along at high speed over the smooth sand belt. He watched till it became a small speck, then turned to the chart table and reached for the star log. He began to make concise entries in a neat steady handwriting.

He had been working for about twenty minutes, when a voice said softly in his ear: *Masumo would speak with Lukas of the sky-machine.*"

Lukas jumped as if he'd been stung. He spun round, but there was no one else on deck. Then he looked through the observation panel, and saw down below a small,

naked figure in the distance. It was coming towards the *Henri Poincaré.* Puzzled, Lukas went down to meet it.

"Did you talk to me while I was in the sky-machine?" he asked abruptly.

But Masumo only smiled, raised his leathery arm in greeting, and offered the traditional salutation in his own language. Lukas returned it, and together they walked back to the ship.

Oddly enough, Lukas had already forgotten about the voice, and did not remember it until much later. Suddenly, he wanted to show Masumo the interior of the ship, wanted to see his reaction to the wonders of terrestrial science.

He gestured towards the ladder. The hominid smiled, and scrambled up it with incredible speed. Lukas followed and began the conducted tour.

If he expected a violent reaction —a dislpay of superstition, dread or near-worship—he was disappointed. Masumo looked at volatility tubes, pile drives, Kirchhausen units, refrigerators, contour berths, electronic cookers and motion picture projectors with the same bland smile. It was as if, thought Lukas, the old hominid was on guard against something—too much on guard to remember that he ought to be suitably astounded.

Only once did Masumo forget himself. They were on the navigation deck, and Lukas had just shown him the manual telescope, pointing it towards the forest line and letting him look through. But even the glass that made things magically near did not shake Masumo. He treated it with that same unwavering smile.

Baffled, Lukas turned his attention to the small transceiver, intending to make radio contact with the tractor and see if Masumo would react to voices that he would recognize. He tried five hundred kilocycles, the agreed frequency, and called repeatedly. But as there was no answer, he concluded that Alsdorf and Chirico were out. working on foot. As Lukas got up from the radio bench, he suddenly saw Masumo staring with poorly repressed excitement at a star chart. He stood still and watched for a moment, noting the quick alert interest and the way Masumo swiftly moved his skinny finger from one constellation to another.

Then, aware that Lukas was staring at him, Masumo seemed to withdraw once more into his role of ignorant savage. The bland smile settled over his face like a mask.

"Masumo, you know what those are, don't you?" demanded Lukas, pointing to the star charts.

But the hominid affected not to understand, and said in his own tongue: "Talk to me, man of the sky. Talk to me of your voyage across the ocean of many suns."

Certain now that Masumo was practicing some elaborate deception, Lukas wanted to shake the truth out of him. Instead, he found himself obeying the old hominid with a strange sense of emotional submission—as if his will-power had been paralyzed.

Masumo left the *Henri Poincaré* a little before sunset—long enough to give him sufficient light to get back to the village. A few minutes after the hominid had gone, Lukas managed to rouse himself from a mental and emotional stupor. He had the sensation of awakening from some peculiar dream. He lit a cigarette, poured himself a stiff drink and tried to consider the events of the afternoon calmly.

He was still puzzling the situation out when Duluth returned from his trip in the monowheel. The engineer found Lukas on the mess-deck, looking—as Duluth remarked—like a pile of ectoplasm left over from a phoney seance.

"What's eating you, Mike? Somebody been making nasty faces through the window?"

Lukas pulled himself together and gave a laconic account of Masumo's visit. Duluth pursed his lips and let out a long low whistle.

"I had a feeling those simple-minded characters were too good to be true," he said slowly. "I got something else for us to think about, as well. In case you haven't noticed it, they never talk to each other. They make plenty of gibberish for our benefit, but they don't use it among themselves. I looked in at shanty-town to say hello on my way back this afternoon. I was there a couple of hours, maybe. There was plenty of noise, all right—and all of it directed at me . . . I thought there was something mighty fishy, but it didn't dawn on me what it was until I was heading back to the ship."

Lukas sat up suddenly. "Joe, you've hit it! These creatures have been taking us for a ride. They're natural telepaths."

Duluth shrugged. "If they're so damn clever, why do they look like a gorilla's next of kin? Why do they live the way they do?"

"That's what we're going to find out."

At that moment, they heard sounds down below indicating that Alsdorf and Chirico had returned with the tractor. Duluth went down to meet them. A few moments later, Alsdorf hurried up the companion ladder. There was a curious, strained look on his face.

"Mike, what is your opinion of witchcraft?" he asked abruptly.

Lukas raised his eyebrows. "I haven't any. You'd better tell me the worst."

The German slumped on to a bench. His gaze fell on the newly opened bottle of whisky. He reached for it, and took a deep draught— straight from the bottle. Lukas was intrigued. This was the first time he had ever seen Alsdorf lose his smooth sang-froid.

"Palladium and platinum deposits," said Alsdorf, coughing a little. "They've completely disappeared."

"What!"

The geophysicist nodded emphatically. "Not a trace . . . They might never have existed . . . Nothing disturbed, no sign of interference. But not a trace of nuggets, ore or any damn thing. . . . Acres and acres of it, Mike, and the whole lot wiped clean out of existence." The shock to his scientific soul was such that he seemed about to burst into tears.

Lukas stared at him. "But the thing is impossible. You're sure—"

Alsdorf slammed the bottle down. "Don't ask me if I'm sure it's the right place. Tony and I nearly went crazy making sure . . . How could it happen, Mike? It's impossible!"

"It *was* impossible, you mean." Lukas stood up. "It looks as if this is our big day, doesn't it?" He gazed through the observation panel at the darkening sky over the forest line, and began to tell Alsdorf about Masumo's visit.

By the time he had finished, the geophysicist had regained control of himself. "Tonight," he said sombrely, "we will make our plans. Tomorrow, we will take the tractor and pay these hominids a visit— with machine pistols, grenades and gas bombs." He laughed mirthlessly. "The experiment will be conducted under scientific conditions. We will see if they are—vulnerable."

"Are you proposing to blast them to glory?" demanded Lukas quietly. "Because if so, you can think again. This is their planet, not ours."

Alsdorf gave him a sour

grin. "Still the adolescent idealist, Mike . . . Why don't you grow up?"

"Don't worry, I'm going," retorted Lukas. "Meanwhile, don't think I'm going to let you intimidate a bunch of defenseless savages."

"I get the impression that they are not so defenseless or so ignorant as we thought," remarked Alsdorf pleasantly. "And while I have no intention of being dramatic, I'm damn well going to find out what's happened to our platinum."

"*Our* platinum?" Lukas stared at him.

"Ours by right of conquest," amended Alsdorf drily. "We have the superior culture, the superior tools and the superior weapons."

Lukas suddenly laughed. "But we aren't telepaths, and we can't do vanishing tricks with large platinum deposits . . . Don't get over-confident, Kurt."

Chirico came up the companion ladder, preceded by a loud blast of invective.

"Those lousy stinking aboriginals! Those sons of a venereal ape! Hi, Mike. I hear you have been having fun, too . . . What beats me is how they could possibly—"

Duluth, who had followed him, said calmly: "I have a theory." The three men turned and stared at him.

Duluth helped himself to a cigarette and lit it. "Yeah," he said with an air of profundity, "they do it with mirrors."

After the evening meal, a formal conference was held on the navi-gation deck. Alsdorf opened it by proposing to make a lightning swoop on the village to capture Masumo, with the logical aim of holding him as a hostage and finding out what he knew. Lukas, as captain of the ship, and therefore the person responsible for the safety of the expedition, promptly vetoed the proposal.

"Are you suggesting, Mike, that we do nothing, that we just hang around waiting to see what happens next?" Alsdorf was scathing.

"Keep your shirt on. Leaving aside the ethics of the thing, I'm merely pointing out that we can't afford to start anything unless we're sure we can finish it. If Masumo is a telepath, we'd be fools to have him in the ship. It's possible he would be able to report back on every move we made."

"Unfortunately," said Chirico with a wry smile, "Mike happens to be right. We do not know how these—these primitive poltergeists operate . . . But, hell, we have to do *something*, don't we?"

"Why not jet out of here and touch down somewhere else?" asked Duluth lazily. "Anything for a quiet life."

Alsdorf withered him with a glance. "And lose the finest platinum deposits we're ever likely to see?"

"Correct me if I'm wrong," drawled Duluth, "but haven't we already lost 'em?"

Glancing quickly from face to face, Lukas could see that the expedition's morale had reached a crucial phase. While he personally would have gladly accepted Duluth's suggestion, for some reason that he could not yet fully understand, he realized that it was psychologically unsound. For the first time in history, a space crew had come up against a quasi-human culture—one that was both beyond and below its terrestrial equivalent—and they could not, with self-respect, ignore its challenge. To do so would be to admit that their own sense of superiority was hollow. And Lukas was dimly aware that if human beings were to realize that they could be beaten by a different kind of creature, with a different concept of power, it would be as big a shock as the original discovery that Earth was not the fixed centre of the universe.

He looked at the faces of his companions, and offered the compromise he had decided upon at the beginning.

"Kurt would like to get tough with the hominids," he said slowly, "but we agree that we're not in a position to get tough. Joe suggests pulling up anchor and trying elsewhere. But that is no good, either. Sooner or later, this kind of problem will occur again. We have to try and tackle it here . . . I suggest that, tomorrow, three of us—with defensive arms, if it makes you feel better—take the tractor and pay them a visit. The aim being to try to find a peaceful solution. One thing we do know, the hominids will understand what we are getting at— if they want to understand. If they don't feel like cooperating over the platinum, well, we'll have to think again . . . But this is their territory, and we can't afford to create a situation that might jeopardize the next space crew to get here."

Chirico made up his mind immediately. "That's the best idea yet, Mike. If the hominids really are mind-readers, they'll know we aren't out for trouble; and they might be willing to meet us . . . What do you say, Kurt?"

The geophysicist shrugged. "I think they will laugh at us. But I'm willing to try diplomacy—once."

"It could be interesting," remarked Duluth. "I'm for it—providing I'm not elected to stay behind and guard the ship. If they can knock off the platinum deposits, they might take it into their nuts to have a crack at vanishing the *Poincaré.*"

"That's my responsibility," said Lukas. "You three had better get some sleep, while I take the first watch."

It was late afternoon before the expedition started. Lukas had suggested the delay in case the hominids themselves chose to make a visit. But though a constant watch had been kept on the forest line, no movement had been observed; and it looked as if the hominids were content to rest on their achievements.

Alsdorf's defensive armament consisted of two machine pistols and a box of gas bombs. He stowed himself, the gas bombs and one machine pistol in the tractor's observation turret, while Duluth took the other machine pistol below and sat with Chirico, who was the driver.

Lukas came down the ladder to see them off. He exchanged a few last minute words with Alsdorf, who had decided to ride with the turret hatch open—in case quick action was needed.

"How is the adrenalin, Kurt?"

The geophysicist gave him a thin smile. "I'm not trigger-happy, if that's what you mean."

Lukas grinned. "If they start throwing telepathy at you, don't waste time with the sleep bombs. Get the hell out of there."

"We'll see."

Lukas went to the driver's compartment. "I'll call you on the transceiver, in fifteen minutes, Joe. Don't let them pull any rabbits out of your hat."

Duluth laughed. "Maybe we'll use a little magic ourselves."

Chirico waved, and switched on the engine. Presently, the tractor was lumbering purposefully towards the forest in a dead straight line.

Lukas went back to the navigation deck and settled down to wait and watch. He lit a cigarette and made himself comfortable in the astrodome, thus commanding the view on all sides. There was nothing to be seen. Eventually, he realized it was time for the radio check. He climbed down the short ladder and switched the transceiver on.

"Ship to tractor, ship to tractor. Have you made contact yet?"

"Tractor to ship." Lukas recognized Duluth's voice. "Tractor to ship. We hit shanty-town a couple of minutes ago. Kurt is raising his blood pressure trying to make Masumo understand what he's talking about. The old son of an ape is playing stupid. Looks as if he's enjoying it, too . . . Any developments your end?"

"Dead quiet. I hope it stays that way . . . I'll leave this set on receive, then you can call me any time."

"O. K. Mike. This is the picture so far. The old boy wanted to take Kurt into one of those adobe shacks—a bit bigger than the rest. It looks like some kind of council chamber. But Kurt wasn't having any. So he and Masumo are standing just in front of the tractor. The louder Kurt shouts, the more the old boy seems to like it. At the moment, he's calmly drawing patterns in the sand with a pointed stick. You know, they look just like star maps . . . Yep, they are star maps! Mike, can you believe this—he's plotted our course for a Solar deceleration! Now Kurt has really lost his temper. Any moment now, he'll start tossing something . . . Hey, Kurt! For Chrissake—"

Suddenly, Duluth's voice was cut off. Lukas felt the sweat forming on his forehead. Immediately, he threw the switch to transmit.

"Ship to tractor! Joe! What's happened? Are you receiving me?"

There was no background noise—
nothing.

Lukas stared dully at the transceiver trying to work out all possibilities. Mechanical failure was
possible, but least likely. Something
had blasted the transmission.

Minutes went by, and nothing
happened. Lukas hauled himself up
into the astrodome and gazed intently on all sides. The landscape
was as empty as ever. He went down
and tried the transceiver again, but
his calls were unanswered. He tried
to decide what to do. But all the
plans he devised were blocked by the
basic fact that he must not leave the
ship unguarded. That would be the
final stupidity. Again, he tried the
transceiver, and again there was no
response. He could only wait and
hope.

Meanwhile, the sun moved slowly down the yellowish sky until it
hung over the forest. Mechanically,
Lukas swung himself up into the
astrodome for the twentieth time
and looked round. Then he saw
something moving, and grabbed the
telescope.

He couldn't believe his eyes. The
tractor was half way across the sand
belt, heading straight for the *Henri
Poincaré*. Sitting crosslegged in
front of its turret, rocking gently
with the tractor's motion, and looking like a somnolent toad, was
Masumo.

Lukas jumped down from the
dome. Simultaneously, he knew that
everything had gone wrong, and yet
somehow it was all right.

Then he heard a voice speak softly in his ear: *"Be not afraid, man
of the sky-machine. I come in
peace."*

Against all reason—even against
his will—Lukas laid down the machine pistol he had just picked up,
and felt the tension drain out of
him. The words had reacted on him
not as a command but as a compul-
sion. Calmly, he went down the
companion ladder and out of the
space ship. He stood on the still
warm sand, watching the tractor
draw near.

It pulled up smoothly; and at the
same time, Masumo stood up,
jumped lightly from the turret and
raised his hand in the customary
greeting. On his face was a fixed
bland smile.

Lukas almost ignored him. His attention was riveted to the tractor.

Chirico was sitting at the wheel,
stiff as a ramrod, gazing fixedly
ahead with a vacancy of expression
that seemed to suggest a state of
hypnosis. Duluth, his eyes open, his
brain still working, had slumped on
his seat in a catatonic stupor. Alsdorf
lay quietly on the floor, curled up
in a tight foetal ball.

With a sudden blaze of anger,
Lukas turned to Masumo, raising
his arm for a crushing blow. Then
he saw the expression in the old
hominid's eyes; and his arm
dropped impotently to his side.

It was as if the landscape had
darkened; as if Masumo had somehow become luminous; as if he had
grown taller than the ship. As if

his head had suddenly filled the sky.

Lukas gazed at the eyes, fascinated. They became lakes, then whirlpools of infinite depth, drawing him down. Masumo's smile did not change, his lips did not move, but the voice spoke once more.

It was a calm, quiet voice. And yet, the voice of thunder.

"Man-of-the-sky, you came to my village, and I read your heart. I saw there the picture of your machine-made civilization, its dreams of conquest, its nightmares of fear.

"Your people are but children. We can allow them to play a little longer. But presently, they must put away their childish toys. Presently, they must learn to take their place as a single world-spirit in the star culture of immortals.

"Men live and die. But the racial purpose is beyond time. We of this world had learned to surrender to that purpose, to become one with all world-spirits throughout the vast pattern of stars, before your people could stand upright on two feet.

"Someday, your race will find itself, and freely follow the universal destiny. We, the enlightened ones, whom you have chosen to see only as ignorant savages, will await you. Until then, it is our task to see that you do not plunder the stars too much . . .

"Suspecting the reason for your visit, Man-of-the-sky, we tested you and your companions with the rare metals you desire. And thus we learned how far you have yet to travel to reach enlightenment . . .

"You will leave this planet now. When you are voyaging through the dark oceans of the sky, your companions will recover. But neither they nor you will remember these happenings. You will know only that the journey was futile, that the planet was barren of all you sought . . . Farewell, Man-of-the sky. May your people reach the ultimate tranquility in which diverse worlds—greater in number than the sands of the sea—have found their common end."

Suddenly, Masumo seemed to return to his normal stature. He raised his arm once more to Lukas, lightly touched the centre of his forehead, then turned and walked slowly away over the sand belt towards the dark line of the forest.

Lukas watched until the hominid was no more than a moving speck. Then, like a remotely controlled automaton, he went to the tractor.

Presently, some time after the sun had set, the *Henri Poincaré* emitted a jet of green flame from its planetary drive. Swiftly, it began to climb in a blinding arc until, moving up into the reaches of sunlight again, its path was etched like a bow of burning gold.

In the few seconds before it passed beyond the visible range, it was observed from the surface of Fomalhaut Three by eyes that were no longer dark and without lustre. Eyes that radiated an incomprehensible power, that glowed like twin diamonds, that burned like bright, binary stars.

in

lonely

lands

by ... Harlan Ellison

When you'd lived so long in
the shadows, as he had done,
you waited anxiously for the
coming of the Grey Man...

*"He clasps the crag
    with crooked hands;
"Close to the sun
    in lonely lands,
"Ring'd with the azure
    world he stands."*
ALFRED, LORD TENNYSON

PEDERSON knew night was falling; the harp crickets had come out.
The halo of sun's warmth that had
kept him golden through the long
day had dissipated, and he could
feel the chill of the darkness now.
Despite his blindness there was an
appreciable *changing* in the shadows that lived where sight had once
long ago been.

"Pretrie," he called into the hush,
and the answering echoes from the
moon valleys answered and answered, "Pretrie, Pretrie, Pretrie," down
and down, almost to the foot of the
small mountain.

"I'm here, Pederson old man.
What do you want of me?"

The silken overtones of the
alien's voice were soothing. Though
Pederson had never seen the tall,
utterly ancient Jilkite, he had passed
his arthritic, spatulate fingers over
the alien's hairless, teardrop head,
had seen by feeling the deep round

*The fact that it is difficult to find three people in any SF gathering who
will agree on Harlan Ellison is obvious testimony to his impact on the field.
He will be remembered for his* SOLDIER FROM TOMORROW *(FU, August 1957),
and is the author of the recently published novel,* RUMBLE *(Pyramid, 35¢).*

sockets where eyes glowed, the pug nose, the thin, lipless gash that was mouth. Pederson knew this face as he knew his own, with its wrinkles and sags and protruberances. He knew the Jilkite was so old no man could estimate it in Earth years.

"Do you hear the Grey Man coming yet?"

Pretrie sighed, a lung-deep sigh, and Pederson could hear the inevitable crackling of bones as the alien hunkered down beside the old man's pneumorack.

"He comes but slowly, old man. But he comes. Have patience."

"Patience," Pederson chuckled ruminatively. "I got that, Pretrie. I got that and that's about all. I used to have time, too, but now that's about gone. You say he's coming?"

"Coming, old man. Time. Just time."

"How are the blue shadows, Pretrie?"

"Thick as fur in the moon valleys, old man. Night is coming."

"Are the moons out?"

There was a breathing through wide nostrils — ritualistically slit nostrils — and the alien replied, "Only two this night. Tayseff and Teei are below the horizon. It grows dark swiftly. Perhaps this night old man."

"Perhaps," Pederson agreed.

"Have patience."

Pederson had not always had patience. As a young man, the blood warm in him, he had fought with his Presby-Baptist father, and taken to space. He had not believed in Heaven, Hell, and the accompanying rigors of the All-Church. Not then. Later, but not then.

To space he had gone, and the years had been good to him. He had aged slowly, healthily, as men do in the dark places between dirt. Yet he had seen the death, and the men who had died believing, the men who had died not believing. And with time had come the realization that he was alone, and that some day, one day, the Grey Man would come for him.

He was always alone, and in his loneliness, when the time came that he could no longer tool the great ships through the star-spaces, he went away.

He went away and found Jilka, where the days were warm and the nights were mild. For blindness had found him, and the slowness that forewarned him of the Grey Man's visit. Blindness from too many glasses of vik and scotch, from too much hard radiation, from too many years of squinting into the vastnesses. Blind, and unable to earn his keep.

So alone, he had found Jilka; as the bird finds the tree, as the winter-starved deer finds the last bit of bark, as the water quenches the thirst. He had found it, there to wait for the Grey Man, and it was there that the Jilkite Pretrie had found him.

They sat together, silently, on the

porch with many things unsaid, yet passing between them.

"Pretrie?"

"Old man."

"I never asked you what you get out of this. I mean—"

Pretrie reached and the sound of his claw tapping the formica table-top came to Pederson. Then the alien was pressing a bulb of water-diluted vik into his hand. "I know what you mean, old man. I have been with you close on two harvestings. I am here. Does that not satisfy you?"

Two harvestings. Equivalent to four years Earth-time, Pederson knew. The Jilkite had come out of the dawn one day, and stayed to serve the old blind man. Pederson had never questioned it. One day he was struggling with the coffee pot (he dearly loved old-fashion brewed coffee and scorned the use of the coffee briquettes) and the heat controls on the hutch . . . the next he had an undemanding, un-selfish manservant who catered with dignity and regard to his every de-sire. It had been a companionable relationship; he had made no great demands on Pretrie, and the alien had asked nothing in return.

He was in no position to wonder or question.

Though he could hear Pretrie's brothers in the chest-high floss brakes at harvesting time, still the Jilkite never wandered far from the hutch.

Now, it was nearing its end.

"It has been easier with you here.

I—uh—thanks, Pretrie," the old man felt the need to say it clearly, without embroidery.

A soft grunt of acknowledg-ment. "I thank you for allowing me to remain with you, old man, Peder-son," the Jilkite answered softly.

A spot of cool touched Peder-son's cheek. At first he thought it was rain, but no more came, and he asked, "What was that?"

The Jilkite shifted—with what Pederson took for discomfort—and answered, "A custom of my race."

"What?" Pederson persisted.

"A tear, old man. A tear from my eye to your body."

"Hey, look . . ." he began, trying to convey his feelings, and realizing *look* was the wrong word. He stumbled on, an emotion coming to him he had long thought dead in-side himself. "You don't have to be —uh—you know, sad, Pretrie. I've lived a good life. The Grey Man doesn't scare me." His voice was brave, but it cracked with the age in the cords.

"My race does not know sadness, Pederson. We know gratitude and companionship and beauty. But not sadness. That is a serious lack, so you have told me, but we do not yearn after the dark and the lost. My tear is a thank you for your kindness."

"Kindness?"

"For allowing me to remain with you."

The old man subsided then, waiting. He did not understand. But the alien had found him, and the presence of Pretrie had made things easier for him in these last years. He was grateful, and wise enough to remain silent.

They sat there thinking their own thoughts, and Pederson's mind winnowed the wheat of incidents from the chaff of life spent.

He recalled the days alone in the great ships, and how he had at first laughed to think of his father's religion, his father's words about loneliness: "No man can walk the road without companionship, Will," his father had said. He had laughed, declaring he was a loner, but now, with the unnameable warmth and presence of the alien here beside him, he knew the truth.

His father had been correct.

It was good to have a friend. Especially when the Grey Man was coming. Strange how he knew it with such calm certainty, but that was the way of it. He knew, and he waited placidly.

After a while, the chill came down from the High Blue Mountains, and Pretrie brought out the treated shawl. He laid it about the old man's thin shoulders, where it clung with warmth, and hunkered down on his triple-jointed legs once more.

"I don't know, Pretrie," Pederson ruminated, later.

There was no answer. There had been no question.

"I just don't know. Was it worth it all? The time aspace, the men I've known, the lonely ones who died and the dying ones who were never lonely."

"All peoples know that ache, old man," Pretrie philosophized. He drew a deep breath.

"I never thought I needed anyone. I've learned better, Pretrie."

"One never knows." Pederson had taught the alien little; Pretrie had come to him speaking English. It had been one more puzzling thing about the Jilkite, but again Pederson had not questioned it. There were many missionaries and spacers in this sector of the Rim.

"Everybody needs somebody," Pederson went on.

"You will never know," Pederson agreed in emphasis. Then added, "Perhaps you will."

Then the alien stiffened, his claw upon the old man's arm. "He comes, Pederson old man."

A thrill of expectancy, and a shiver of near-fright came with it. Pederson's grey head lifted, and despite the warmth of the shawl he felt cold. So near now. "He's coming?"

"He is here."

They both sensed it, for Pederson could feel the awareness in the Jilkite beside him; he had grown sensitive to the alien's moods, even as the other had plumbed his own. "The Grey Man," Pederson spoke the words softly on the night air, and the moon valleys did not respond.

"I'm ready," said the old man, and he extended his left hand for the grasp. He set down the bulb of vik with his other hand.

The feel of hardening came stealing through him, and it was as though someone had taken his hand in return. Then, as he thought he was to go, alone, he said, "Good-bye to you, Pretrie, friend."

But there was no good-bye from the alien beside him. Instead, the Jilkite's voice came to him as through a fog softly descending.

"We go together, friend Pederson. The Grey Man comes to all races. Why do you expect me to go alone? Each need is a great one.

"I am here, Grey Man. Here. I am not alone." Oddly, Pederson knew the Jilkite's claw had been offered, and taken in the clasp.

He closed his blind eyes.

After a great while, the sound of the harp crickets thrummed high once more, and on the porch before the hutch, there was the silence of peace.

Night had come to the lonely lands; night, but not darkness.

STATEMENT REQUIRED BY THE ACT OF AUGUST 24, 1912, AS AMENDED BY THE ACTS OF MARCH 3, 1933, AND JULY 2, 1946 (Title 39, United States Code, Section 233) SHOWING THE OWNERSHIP, MANAGEMENT, AND CIRCULATION OF Fantastic Universe, published bi-monthly at New York, N. Y., for October 1, 1958.

1. The names and addresses of the publisher, editor, and business manager are: Publisher, King-Size Publications, Inc., 320 Fifth Avenue, New York 1, N. Y.; Editor, Hans S. Santesson, 320 Fifth Avenue, New York 1, N. Y.; Business Manager, George Shapiro, 54 East 8th Street, New York 3, N. Y.

2. The owner is: (If owned by a corporation, its name and address must be stated and also immediately thereunder the names and addresses of stockholders owning or holding 1 percent or more of total amount of stock. If not owned by a corporation, the names and addresses of the individual owners must be given. If owned by a partnership or other unincorporated firm, its name and address, as well as that of each individual member, must be given.) King-Size Publications, Inc., 320 Fifth Avenue, New York 1, N. Y.; H. L. Herbert, 969 Park Avenue, New York 28, N. Y.; George Shapiro, 54 East 8th Street, New York 3, N. Y.

3. The known bondholders, mortgagees, and other security holders owning or holding 1 percent or more of total amount of bonds, mortgages, or other securities are: (If there are none, so state.) None.

4. Paragraphs 2 and 3 include, in cases where the stockholder or security holder appears upon the books of the company as trustee or in any fiduciary relation, the name of the person or corporation for whom such trustee is acting; also the statements in the two paragraphs shows the affiant's full knowledge and belief as to the circumstances and conditions under which stockholders and security holders who do not appear upon the books of the company as trustees, hold stock and securities in a capacity other than that of a bona fide owner.

5. The average number of copies of each issue of this publication sold or distributed, through the mails or otherwise, to paid subscribers during the 12 months preceding the date shown above was: (This information is required from daily, weekly, semiweekly, and triweekly newspapers only.)

GEORGE SHAPIRO,
Business Manager.

[SEAL]

Sworn to and subscribed before me this 9th day of September, 1958.
WALTER S. COOPER,
Notary Public.

State of New York. Qualified in New York County, No. 31-5811250. Cert. filed in N. Y. Co. Clks. & Term expires March 30, 1960.

time

to

change

by ... Bertram Chandler

There had always been a
Party and there'd always
been The Boss. And there
had always been Them...

JONES took his time in making
his way to the address that Wilberforce had given him. He took a deliberately roundabout route, using
all the usual tricks—and a few that
weren't quite so usual—to shake off
any possible followers. Not that
Jones thought that he was being
followed—but, having once been a
member of the Force himself, he
possessed a healthy respect for the
methods and capabilities of the
Police.

It had been, of course, his dis-
missal from the Force that had
turned him against the System. The
rank injustice of it all still rankled;
he still did not see how the Inspect-
or could have considered himself
entitled to half the bribe that he,
Jones—then a Constable First Class
—had received for conniving at the
escape of the little black marketeer
on his way to jail. The Inspector,
of course, was a full member of the
Party and Jones was only a Pro-
bationer. He would never be a Party
Member now.

It was Wilberforce—he, like
Jones, was a tank cleaner in the em-
ploy of the Sewerage Conversion
Commission—who had first put
Jones in touch with the Under-

*There is a subtly ironic quality to the writing of Bertram Chandler—
even in the present story—which has perhaps disturbed some anthologists.
It is an interesting quality however, evidenced in his* FALL OF KNIGHT *(FU,
June 1958) and also in his earlier* SENSE OF WONDER *(FU, February 1958).*

ground. Jones, naturally, had thought at first of turning informer, of selling his information at a price that would include re-instatement, promotion and full Party membership. Wilberforce—who had long, and sometimes hazardous, years as a recruiting officer behind him had foreseen this reaction. He reminded Jones that the arm of the Underground was long, that informers almost invariably came to bad ends, to spectacularly bad ends. Jones, the ex-policeman, knew this. He himself had heard a man scream, had seen him fall to the Station floor writhing in agony while his dissolving entrails poured from his mouth in a sickening flood. He did not know how it was done, nobody in the Force knew how it was done. The most widely accepted theory was that the informer had been given some poison that, somehow, was harmless until bombarded with radiation at a certain frequency. And Jones, never a man to turn down anything that was free, had often accepted both food and drink from Wilberforce's lunch pail.

There had been meetings, of course, which Jones had attended. Masks had been worn by all those present and, in other ways, the strictest secrecy had been observed. There had been speeches—and it had been the speeches that had aroused Jones' contempt. He could understand revenge as a motivation —it was the lust for revenge that had brought him into the Underground. But all the talk of the hap-

pier days of the past, all the talk of the possibility of happier days in the future, was, to Jones, mere fantasy and not very entertaining fantasy at that. There had always been a Party. There had always been The Boss. There had always been an Underground and, too, there was always the chance that the Underground might one day defeat the Party—why, else, should the Force maintain its unceasing vigilance? And, if the Underground should, at last, be victorious then it, in its turn, would be the Party, and there was at least a fair chance that one Jones would be the new Chief of Police.

It was after one of these meetings that Wilberforce—who, throughout, had acted as Jones' sponsor— had asked Jones to stay behind. The two men sat on their hard bench, watching the others leave the drab room by ones and twos and threes. Jones—once a policeman, always a policeman—studied them as they walked by, trying hard to memorize any clues to indentity although, masked and cloaked as the Underground members were, there was little to memorize but stature and peculiarities of gait.

Wilberforce laughed.

"It's no good, Jones. Even if you knew that the tall man who's just gone out was, say, John Smith, a comptometer operator for the Astronautics Commission (he's not, of course—even I don't know who he is) the knowledge would be of no use to you, or to your late employers. We've taken more trouble with

you than with the average recruit—
and you'd be dead, painfully, before
you got to within a hundred yards
of a telephone booth, let alone a
Police Station . . ."

"Why should I be important?"
asked Jones, feeling a little flattered.

"That you'll be finding out shortly," replied the other. "But we're
alone now. Come through to the
back room."

There were three people in the
back room—two men and a woman.
They were wearing neither masks
nor cloaks. Their clothing was plain,
but not cheap. They were, decided
Jones, members of the dwindling
class of non-Party technicians.

"You can remove your masks,"
said the woman, in a high, clear
voice.

She was young, in her early
thirties apparently, although there
were strands of grey in her close
cropped black hair. Her face had a
hard handsomeness. Her mouth was
wide and mobile, but her lips were
thin.

"So this is the famous Mr. Jones,"
said the fat, bald man on her right.
"Even though he looks and smells
like a sewage worker he still carries
the Police College stamp. Height—
a little above average. Hair—mousy.
Eyes—could be grey—could be
brown. Face—strong, but not too
strong; intelligent, but not too intelligent. I often wonder if they
breed these policemen especially for
the job . . ."

"Cut out the theorizing, Bill,"
said the other man, who was tall
and grey haired and was so thin as
to suggest malnutrition. "Here's the
tool that Wilberforce has found for
us. He passed through the Police
College, so has all the qualities we
need. He hates the System. We
needn't worry about his motives."

"I *do*," said the fat man. "I *do*.
There's one tenet I never accept—
that the end justifies the means . . ."

"Shut up!" snapped the woman.
"William Jones," she went on, "you
have seen our faces. We know that
you will sell us if you think that
there is the slightest chance of your
getting away with it. Let me assure
you, now, that there is not. Let me
assure you, too, that your knowledge
of our physical appearance is quite
valueless. Look!"

She got to her feet. There was a
slight clumsiness, an almost un-
noticeable stiffness in her motions
that did not escape Jones, the trained
observer. She put one long fingered
hand on either side of the fat man's
head. She twisted it. It turned, un-
screwing. She stood facing Jones
across the wide table, the head in
her hands.

"You are privileged, Jones," said
the fat man. "Not many members
of the Underground are privileged
to witness this demonstration. Usually new members never know that
they are being interviewed by three
remotely controlled robots—which
robots, I need hardly tell you, bear
not the slightest resemblance to us.
This, usually, is our way of weed-
ing out potential informers. They

rush to the nearest Police Station to blab out a full description of the mysterious Triumvirate. The description they give is, of course, useless; the Police arrive at the house where the interview has been held just too late to put out the fire—and the informer is . . . eliminated. But we don't want *you* eliminated. As you know, Wilberforce has taken great pains throughout to prevent you from turning informer."

"That is so," said Jones, addressing the fat man's head.

He was relieved when the woman screwed it back on to the body.

"You can be of great assistance to us," said the woman. "You can overthrow the System. I need hardly say that you will be suitably rewarded."

"You will want a Chief of Police," said Jones.

"Shall we?" Thin eyebrows flickered upwards in a gesture of interrogation. "Shall we? But never mind—we have a job for you to do —a job for which you will be, as we said, suitably rewarded."

"What is it?" asked Jones.

"To kill the Boss," said the thin man.

Jones swallowed.

"You might as well kill me now," he said, a little wildly. "It'll be faster—and far less painful. You picked the right man for the job all right —you picked a man who knows how utterly impossible it is."

"We don't want you to kill him *now*," said the woman.

"It makes no difference," said Jones. "I'm telling you—and I should know—that it's impossible. Furthermore—just suppose that I do get through the Outer Guards and the Inner Guards, through the network of defensive devices . . . What then? I shoot a man, or I stab him, or I strangle him. He *looks* like the Boss. But is he? How many doubles has he got? You don't know, even the Police don't know. And even if I get the right one—I haven't killed the Party."

"We know that," said the woman patiently. "We're prepared to admit, Jones, that you, as a Police College graduate, have made a study of the art of putting down revolution. We, of the Underground, have made a study of the art of revolution itself. We know that *at this stage* the destruction of a figurehead would be worse than useless, would, in all probability, lead to an intensified effort on the part of the Police that would stamp out the Underground for all time. After all —an Underground existing only on paper, only in the minds of the masses, would be just as useful to the Authorities as one existing in actuality—and far less dangerous.

"Anyhow—*we* have decided when the Boss is to be killed. You will be able to do it with no danger to yourself whatsoever—well, there will be danger, but it will be slight. You must have been exposed to far greater danger many a time when you were a Policeman."

It's only a robot talking, thought Jones, but there is a real woman behind the scenes somewhere. It may be her real voice that I am hearing. If it is—then I'm fairly certain that she is speaking the truth.

He said aloud, "All right. You've almost convinced me. But you'll have to tell me more — much more . . ."

"Later," said the fat man. "You will share Wilberforce's lunch, as usual, tomorrow. He will tell you a time, and an address. That is all."

There was an audible click, and all semblance of life left the three robots. Quietly Wilberforce and Jones left the room, left the house, made their way out into the dark, dreary street. Silently a monocar swept towards them, the blinding beam of its searchlight lingering over the two men. It was a police car, and Jones felt the urge to hail it, to demand to be taken to the nearest Station where he could tell his story.

"You'd better not," said Wilberforce quietly.

The car passed and hummed away into the distance. Jones and Wilberforce walked half a mile through the thin drizzle to the nearest bus stop.

Jones took a roundabout route to the address that Wilberforce had given him. It was in a street just inside the Inner City limits, but he took a helicopter bus to one of the outer suburbs, then a train to another suburb, walked a mile to a bus stop and so made his way back to the city. There was the business of a change of clothing in a public lavatory and the insertion of a tiny pebble into his right shoe to produce a convincing limp, there was the putting on of a pair of heavily rimmed spectacles with plain lenses. There was—but this was elemental —the deliberate mingling with crowds and the equally deliberate walking along interminable straight stretches of empty street.

The shop for which he was looking was in a street of shops. It was sandwiched between a branch of the People's Bank and Lottery and a branch of the People's Pearl Emporium. Jones spent a little time studying the lists of winning numbers in the last lottery, then transferred his attention to the show of cultured pearls on their dusty black velvet backings, reflecting that the pearl was, after all, the least interesting of precious stones, even though only the wives and mistresses of Party Members could ever wear them. He wondered how big a reward he would get for the job . . . Marie, he remembered, had wanted pearls and had transferred her affection to the Sergeant who could buy them for her.

The clock over the watchmaker's shop a few doors down told him the time—1745 hours, time for the rendezvous.

And not before time, thought Jones. In spite of the importance of his task he was more than a little inclined to resent the waste of his free afternoon.

He glanced up and down the street—it was one that he had

known well enough in his more affluent days, before his discharge from the Force. He was glad that he had had the forethought to change into a tan tunic and slacks, and was not wearing the dungarees that were almost a compulsory uniform for members of the laboring classes whether on or off duty. Two girls were looking into the window of the Pearl Emporium, now, and an elderly man was studying the lottery results. Jones knew none of them, not even by sight.

Casually he entered the door of the shop.

It was, as he had known, a radio dealer's establishment. It was owned by a member of the still-existing class of small shopkeepers and artisans, one of the people who functioned more efficiently as free individuals than as employees of one of the huge Commissions. Jones knew the man, had often collected "protection money" from him. As he studied a display of wall television units, trying to assume the air of a possible purchaser, he wondered if the man would recognize him.

The shopkeeper came, walking silently, from somewhere at the back. Recognition flickered in his eyes, but he said nothing to indicate that he knew Jones.

"Can I help you, sir?" he asked.

"I'm interested in historical films," said Jones. "A Mr. Trenton said that you might be able to help me."

"Historical films . . ." said the shopkeeper. "We have none out

here, sir. If you would step round to the back . . ."

"Certainly," said Jones. "I have the time."

He followed the shopkeeper, along a passage, down a flight of stairs, into a cellar. When he saw the mass of complex apparatus—the coils and the vacuum tubes, the meters and the heavy chair with its straps and electrodes—he almost recoiled in horror, reached for the pistol that he no longer carried. It was all far too much like something in the cellars of Police Headquarters.

"Don't worry, Jones," said the shopkeeper, departing from the ritual of word and counterword that, up till now, the two of them had been observing. "Don't worry—there's nothing lethal or even painful here. Not that I wouldn't enjoy doing to you what you've done to some of my friends."

"Don't waste any time," said Jones virtuously. "I'm here to do a job for your bosses—and you're supposed to help me."

"There's no rush, Jones," replied the shopkeeper. "You have to be put into the picture before you can do anything. Sit on that box—a little oil on your trousers won't matter—and I'll tell you what this is all about." He waited until Jones, having spread a handkerchief over the not very clean top of the box, was seated, then went on. "What do you know of history, Jones?"

"What everybody knows. Almost since Man first appeared on this world the Party has governed. Of the Party only the Boss is immortal. All good comes from the Boss. As he sees fit he presents mankind with new machines—just as, some time in the remote past, he presented them with radio, television, the cinema, the aeroplane . . ."

"You really believe that?" asked the shopkeeper.

"Of course. Everybody does."

"What year is this?" asked the shopkeeper.

"2123," answered Jones. "Two thousand, one hundred and twenty three years since the Boss appeared to lead men upward from savagery."

"And yet," said the other, "you think that you can kill the Boss . . ."

"Of course. I used to be in the Force—don't forget that. I know the lengths that are gone to to protect the Boss from his enemies. He must be mortal—at least insofar as violence is concerned. And he must be old. He must be—otherwise he would not let injustice flourish the way that it does . . ."

"You must miss your cut of the protection money," said the shopkeeper.

"I do," said Jones, then realized that he did not like, had never liked, the little, dried-up, white haired man. He lapsed into sullen silence.

"So you think that if we had a change of Bosses you might better yourself," suggested the old man.

"Yes," said Jones sullenly.

"We must use such tools as come to hand," said the shopkeeper. "We've used other tools before you, Jones—but they . . . vanished.

They were members of the criminal classes and, doubtless, they are doing quite nicely for themselves where we sent them. What we really wanted for the job was somebody like yourself—somebody versed in criminal procedure and with a strong motive for revenge . . ."

"Revenge *and* reward," said Jones.

"All right, if you want it that way. Now, Jones, I'm going to give you a history lesson. What I tell you you won't believe—but you'll have the proof of it soon enough. First of all—the Boss is not the Boss; not the original Boss, I mean. The first one, after he rose to power, had his doubles. The Party has seen to it that there is always a double to take over, to make the necessary public appearances. When necessary, plastic surgery has been used. But—there is always a man with the Boss's face, figure and manner, always apparently in his middle forties, to act as a figurehead."

"Rubbish," said Jones. "The Party scientists could confer immortality on anybody—that is if the Boss let them have the secret."

"Have it your own way—but let me carry on with the history lesson. It was in 1973 that the first Boss came to power. There had been a war in which atomic weapons had been used and, furthermore, hostilities had been followed by widespread economic collapse. Conditions were ripe for any demagogue who could promise peace and plenty. The Boss—Howard Poindexter was his name—was such a demagogue, you know."

"I can't believe it," said Jones.

"Here's proof," said the old man. He got up from the box on which he was sitting, walked to a cupboard against the wall. He opened it, took out a bundle of yellowed paper. "Newspapers," he said. "At one time news was disseminated by the printed word as well as by radio. It was, in its way, inconvenient— a record existed of any mis-statement, any broken promise, made by any politician. Once the People's Party rose to power newspapers were suppressed. The rewriting of the history books soon followed. The People's Party started by controlling the present—then they turned their attention to the past. Every record giving the lie to their official histories has been destroyed. Well —not *every* record. We've saved some."

Jones took the flimsy sheets that the old man had called newspapers. He looked at the date on one of them—March 5, 1973. He read the big black type: PEOPLE'S PARTY SWEEPS TO POWER IN SOUTH. POINDEXTER PROMISES PEACE AND PLENTY. There was a photograph there, blurred and faded by time. It showed a man standing on some sort of platform addressing a huge crowd. The man was the Boss.

"You could have printed these yesterday," said Jones.

"I suppose we could. But look at the age of the paper. See how brittle it is."

"Chemicals, radiation . . . I don't know. I'm a Policeman, not a chemist."

"You *were* a Policeman. And you want to murder the Boss. You'll have to put yourself in my hands if you want to do it. Sit there and read these books and newspapers while I get things ready. It's essential that you have a clear picture of the time to which you're going."

"*Time?*" demanded Jones. "*Place,* you mean."

He read the newspapers. They were, he had to admit, masterly jobs of faking. They told him of some mythical age in which men had possessed the unheard power of electing their governors. They hinted at a standard of living for the laboring classes that was, by Jones' standards, utterly fantastic—and this in a world that had been devastated by war and brought to ruin by economic collapse. Jones turned to the books. There was one, by an author named Wells, called THE OUTLINE OF HISTORY. Jones skimmed through the yellowed pages, read a paragraph here and there, looked at the illustrations. The whole thing was utterly fantastic. It could not be fact. It could not possibly be fact. It must be some ancient imaginative novel written in the form of a history book.

"Are you ready?" asked the old man.

Jones started.

"I suppose so. Where are you sending me?"

"I'm not sending you *anywhere*. You've heard of Time Travel?"

"Yes," said Jones. "Gossip gets around. Some of the scientists working for the Commission of Physics claim to have sent a mouse back three seconds in time . . ."

"The Party doesn't have all the scientists," said the shopkeeper. "The Underground has them too. I'm one of them. This shop gives me the excuse to buy and to make all sorts of apparatus. *I* sent a mouse back in time *five* seconds thirty years ago. Now, I can send a man back one hundred and fifty years.

"Take this thing like a wristwatch. Strap it on—either wrist will do. When you wish to return to the here and now, press the knob at the side. Take this pistol—it's a Schultzer automatic, fully loaded. I needn't tell you what *that* can do. Now, listen carefully. I am going to send you back in time. You will find yourself in this cellar—the building is over one hundred and fifty years old. Make your way out into the street as unobtrusively as possible. It shouldn't be hard—clothing styles have changed hardly at all since the Party came to power. (There was rather more color in those days, I think . . .) Don't be in a hurry—loaf around and get the feel of things. There's some money here . . ." the shopkeeper handed Jones some filthy, unfamiliar looking bills— they did not bear the likeness of the Boss ". . . that will suffice for your immediate needs.

"Howard Poindexter—the Boss— will be in the city. He will have his bodyguards, but they will not be very efficient. He will not, yet, have any doubles. Wait for a good chance —then shoot him with as little compunction as you would use in shooting any other criminal (although his major crimes will yet have to be committed . . .). Press the button, and return."

"There's something I don't quite understand," said Jones. "There's a . . . a paradox somewhere . . ."

"No doubt, no doubt. You can tell me all about it when you get back. Now, sit in the chair . . ."

"No!" shouted Jones. "I see what's wrong! If your story is true, by changing the past I shall change the present! I might even wipe myself out of existence."

"You couldn't do that," said the old man. "In order for you to change the past you *must* exist in the present. Even so—I think a little persuasion might help . . ."

The two men who appeared suddenly had their pistols already drawn. Jones knew that he could never pull his from his pocket, and cock it, in time.

He sat in the chair.

As much as he expected anything, he expected pain. He had seen chairs of similar outward appearance in the cellars of Police Headquarters, and had seen them used. But there was no pain. There was no . . . anything.

He had shut his eyes when the old man had pulled the switch. He opened them again as he found himself sprawling on a hard floor. He was in darkness.

There was a moment or so of panic, then Jones saw a rectangle of dim yellow light. It must be, he reasoned, a door—and the light switch must be just inside the door. Cautiously he edged forward, barking his shins on something hard and sharp. Cautiously he negotiated the obstacle. His groping fingers found the switch, depressed it.

He was, as he had been told that he would be, still in the cellar. There was no apparatus in it, merely a few packing cases. On one of them was a large sheet of printed paper. Jones picked it up. Headlines—black and clear against the whiteness of the paper—stared at him. PEOPLE'S PARTY SWEEPS TO POWER IN SOUTH. POINDEXTER PROMISES PEACE AND PLENTY.

So the Underground was right. So their fantastic history was not a tissue of lies. Yet—"I can't believe it," whispered Jones. "I won't believe it."

Carefully he opened the cellar door, carefully he made his way up the steps. He walked softly along the corridor, found himself in the shop. It was not now a radio shop—it was a grocery. Stacked high were cans of food—more food, and in greater variety, than he had seen even in the luxury Free Market shops of the Inner City. The tiers of cans afforded him cover — through a gap he could see a white-

coated salesman talking to a woman customer. Jones patted his pocket to assure himself that his automatic was still there, then strode boldly into the shop, towards the door.

The salesman turned towards him.

"I'll not keep you waiting long, sir."

"Sorry," said Jones. "No time."

He walked out into the street. It was familiar, yet unfamiliar. Most of the buildings were the same, most of the shops—but they had different names, sold different commodities. Too, it had been early evening when he had been sent on his voyage through Time—now, judging by the position of the sun, it lacked only a few minutes of noon.

The people were different, too. There were more of them and, as he had been told they would be, they were more brightly dressed. Their manner was different, too. They walked and talked with what seemed to Jones to be an insolent carelessness. There was a policeman standing at a corner—the uniform had changed very little—and citizens passed him by without, so far as Jones could see, any qualms whatsoever, no evidence of fear. It seemed terribly wrong.

In spite of what he had seen, Jones could not bring himself to approach the police officer. He accosted a portly, middle aged man.

"Excuse me," he said. "I'm looking for a Mr. Howard Poindexter —the . . . politician. I have a message for him. Do you know where I might find him?"

"From out of town, are you?" asked the man. "One of the Boss's mob, huh? You're on the right side, young feller! The Boss is the only man who can bring law and order back to this country. You'll find him at the Grafton . . ."

"The Grafton? Where . . .?"

"On the corner of Smith and Delamaire Streets. You can't miss it. And tell the Boss that one citizen of this town—Wilbur Spratt's the name, sonny—wishes him well!"

"I'll do that," said Jones. "Thanks, Mr. Spratt."

The Grafton, he thought. What is a Grafton? But it must be the building of the Education and Culture Commission . . .

He found the Grafton without any trouble. He read the unfamiliar words, *Grafton Hotel,* sprawled across the facade of the familiar building. He walked boldly into the lobby, decided that it must be an unusually luxurious lodging house, the sort of place that in his day would be reserved for Party Members only. He strode up to the desk.

"Mr. Poindexter," he said to the bored blonde on duty. "I have a message for him."

"You can't ring," she said. "The telephone's broken down. You'll have to go up. You'll have to climb —the elevator's not working. Room 519 fifth floor."

It was strange to be climbing those familiar stairs again. He had climbed (would climb?) them many

a time when he was attending Police College. Little had changed (would change). Things were newer and cleaner, but that was only to be expected.

After he reached the fifth floor Jones paused to recover his breath. He walked slowly and silently to the door numbered 519. He heard voices inside. One of them was familiar. Carefully, Jones tried the door handle. It was not locked. He paused, then removed his right hand from the handle, substituting his left. With his right hand he drew his pistol, slid back the safety catch.

The enormity of what he was about to do weighed ever more heavily upon him. The rumbling voice that he could hear was the Boss's voice, the accent, the tricks of phrase, were the Boss's.

". . . we must grasp the nettle firmly. There must be no turning back now that we have set our shoulders to the wheel . . ."

The Boss had used these very words when addressing the Police Cadets at the passing out ceremony.

This was the Boss. All that the Boss said was true, all that the Party said was true. There had always been a Boss, there always would be a Boss. The Underground had tricked him with their forged scraps of paper, their cleverly faked books, had almost persuaded him to believe in a world that never was, never could have been. They had used some sort of hypnotic technique on him to make him believe their lies.

But the hypnosis wasn't necessary. He had his grievance. He had sworn revenge. He intended to claim the reward—and intended to rise to the top in whatever upheaval followed the overthrow of the System. He would grasp the nettle. (He smiled thinly.) He had set his shoulders to the wheel. There was no turning back.

He stiffened. Somebody was coming along the corridor—it was two uniformed Police Cadets.

"There shouldn't be any trouble about *my* Party Membership," one of them was saying. "After all—my old man's mistress is secretary to the Commissioner for Internal Affairs. You're just unlucky, Bill—you should have chosen parents with some influence . . . Hello! Who's that? What do you want?"

Jones had no compunction about firing upon the uniform. He had learned the lesson of dog eat dog very early in his Police career. His pistol coughed twice, very quietly. He had aimed for the throat—and he was a crack shot—so the cadets died quietly.

Jones flung open the door. (It no longer, he noticed, bore the numerals 519; it carried the sign, in large letters, DIRECTOR OF POLICE STUDIES.) There were four men in the room. One wore the uniform of a Police Commissioner, two—the inevitable guards—were in plain clothes—the fourth was the Boss. The guards were quick—but Jones' gun was already out and ready to fire.

The second bodyguard's pistol was out of its holster when Jones shot him down. The Commissioner had time to loose off one round from his weapon, but it was wild. Then, over the dead men, Jones faced the Boss. He sneered as the Boss begged for his life. He aimed carefully, deliberately, for the stout man's belly. And he pulled the trigger.

Would that thing on his wrist work? He transferred his pistol to his left hand, felt for the little knob with his right index finger. Something smashed with sickening violence against his left wrist, smashing the instrument and knocking his pistol from his grasp. Strong hands pinioned his arms to his side.

He heard a voice say, "What a mess! Well—it all means promotion!"

Another voice said, "Quiet, you fool! The Boss is coming!"

"There is the Boss!" screamed Jones, jerking his head towards the bleeding, still twitching figure on the floor. "There is the Boss!"

"You murdering swine!" snarled the first voice. "Haven't you ever heard of doubles?"

The Boss stepped into Jones' range of vision. He glanced at the bodies of the two guards, of the Police Commissioner, of his double. He looked at Jones as though trying to identify him. At last he shook his head.

"Take him to the cellars," he ordered at last. "We will leave no stone unturned until we find out who is responsible for this dastardly crime!"

"How did we fail?" asked the plump, middle aged woman.

"Carruthers will be able to tell us," answered the mild, clerkish man.

"We hope," added the man who looked like a professional weight lifter.

The door opened and the shop-keeper came into the room.

"Well—what happened?" asked the woman.

"Just this. The Party *has* changed the past."

"Rubbish!" said the mild man.

"It's not rubbish. I had a spy beam on him all the time. At first the past was as our hoarded records show it to have been—and then, as soon as Jones heard Poindexter's voice, it . . . changed. Poindexter was no longer a demagogue who had yet to achieve power, he was already the Boss, and had been for . . . for . . . I don't know for how long. And the old Grafton Hotel, where he was staying, was quite suddenly the headquarters of the Education and Culture Commission, and crawling with Police Cadets. Oh—it was still the past; but the past as believed in by Jones. Not *our* past."

"What then?" asked the woman.

"Jones shot the Boss. And then he was seized by a squad of Police Cadets, and disarmed, and the Return Control broken (although that was accidental). They took him to the cellars. When I left the shop they were still trying to make him talk. Trying? They were making him talk."

"We're safe enough," said the big man. "After all—it was a hundred and fifty years ago."

"Are we safe?" asked the woman. "You're the scientist, Carruthers. Are we safe?"

"I don't know, Mary. They might believe him. If they do—they might take a careful note of dates and times and places. Then it might well be that we shall be stopped before we can start, and that we shall find ourselves in the cells (if we are still alive, that is) with no memories of this conversation, but a perfectly good set of memories covering our arrest, torture and imprisonment . . ."

"If it were going to happen it would have happened already," said the mild man. "Furthermore—the past that Jones is in is the Party's, not ours . . ."

"Suppose there's a fire in my shop?" asked the scientist. "Suppose the books and papers are destroyed? What then? Will *our* past still exist when the last records are finally gone?"

"Then we'd better *do* something about it," said the giant. "Where we've gone wrong with each attempt is in sending a professional killer to do our dirty work for us. We've made the mistake of assuming that Poindexter, in his early beginnings, was as well defended as the Boss is now. One of us will have to go.

Somebody will have to go to whom the real past is *real,* not just a convincing piece of propaganda put out by the Underground . . ."

"Somebody," said the woman, "who will be tempted to steer the ship of history on to what he thinks is the right course. Tell me, Carruthers, in some parallel world that was snuffed out like a candle flame, did we, or four people like us, make a similar decision, and was the name of our emissary Howard Poindexter?"

SATELLITE-BORNE TV?

THE CONVENTIONAL television equipment—camera, control unit, synchronizing generator and power supply—weighs from three to four hundred pounds. We have already developed miniature transistorized television equipment that can be carried by a satellite weighing only a hundred pounds. We have developed a TV camera weighing less than a pound, and a complete camera system that weights only a few ounces more than four pounds.

Electronics engineers and designers with the Dage Television Division of Thompson Products, Inc., have developed a complete camera system including the sync generator, deflection amplifiers, video amplifiers and power supply, weighing a total of four pounds. The lens weighs an additional few ounces. The camera's dimensions are 2⅜ by 5⅜ by 7¾ inches.

An important feature is an automatic electronic brightness control compensating for various levels of illumination over a range of 250 times, which can be raised to 6,000 times with further attachments. The standard TV scanning rate of 525 lines from top to bottom of picture—30 times each second—is used.

The camera is completely transistorized, and considerably more rugged than conventional TV equipment. Specifications call for 7 watts of power, but with the development of a new type of Vidicon pickup tube (a half inch in diameter, incidentally) only five watts may be needed.

Accent on miniaturization has resulted in a situation where a transmitter, weighing less than 25 pounds, and needing only 50 watts of power, can transmit from 500 to 1,000 miles.

Assuming 60-pounds of high-efficiency batteries are carried, the system can have about fifty hours of continuous operation. If a photo-electric triggering device which shuts off the battery supply, given situations A or B, is used, the fifty hours are then stretched to a hundred or more, and further controls can stretch the time still further. All in all, *batteries, camera and transmitter would weigh less than a hundred pounds.*

universe

in

books

by...Hans Stefan Santesson

Comments on the new books
—on novels and anthologies
and on other matters which
may perhaps interest you.

AGAIN we have a decadent East and a rugged frontiersman, come to Philadelphia for help against the marauding Indians, shocked and dismayed by the lack of interest in Frontier affairs and by signs that friends or hirelings of the very men who are behind the Indian raids are high up in affairs back there in the East. . . .

And yet Robert Silverberg succeeds (as he usually does) in telling an exciting story in STEPSONS OF TERRA (Ace Double Novel, 35 cents), as Baird Ewing, seeking help for the planet Corwin, fights Sirian agents and discovers a startling way to end the menace to his home.

The companion novel is Len Wright's story of "the most valuable human in space," A MAN CALLED DESTINY. Some may question the title.

Poul Anderson is the author of two exciting (but slightly less than classic) adventure novels, THE SNOWS OF GANYMEDE and WAR OF THE WING-MEN (Ace Double Novels, 35 cents). THE SNOWS starts on this quiet note—"Three dead men walked

---

A further report on some books of interest to science fiction and fantasy readers—and to others, interested in Ufology—reflecting the many-sided aspects of life and speculative thought in these times; and some comments, by a reader, on Ivan T. Sanderson's MAN-MADE UFO (F.U., September 1958).

---

across the face of hell . . ."; 'nuff said.

WAR OF THE WING-MEN, by far the more interesting of the two, is the story of three earth people marooned in the stone-age culture of the bat-men ("winged barbarians," to quote the publisher's blurb) of the planet Diomedes, with rather disastrous effect on the lives and times of these natives. An extremely interesting conception of an alien culture. Don't miss this.

I believe many people will find Marla Baxter's MY SATURNIAN LOVER (Vantage Press, $2.50) interesting. The author, who is prominent in flying saucer research (but *not* associated with CSI, we hasten to add) describes both her growing awareness of her own inner self and her relations with Alyn, a mysterious young man who is first said to have had contacts with people from other worlds and who is himself, as it turns out, a "Saturnian." The book is illustrated with photographs of a "Saturnian craft" and of some personalities in contactee circles.

Theodore Sturgeon's THE COSMIC RAPE (Dell, 35 cents) explores the possibility of an entirely different kind of alien invasion—an invasion of the minds of men and women, widely scattered and different, mastery of whom can mean dominance over Earth for an alien intelligence.

Extremely interesting.

DEPARTMENT OF REPRINTS. Pyramid Books have done a public service in reprinting Edward E. Smith's classic THE SKYLARK OF SPACE (Pyramid, 35 cents) in a version revised by the author. A topnotch adventure story. — Robert A. Heinlein's WALDO: GENIUS IN ORBIT (Avon, 35 cents) is a reprint of Heinlein's WALDO AND MAGIC, INC., described by the publishers as "something of a modern science fiction classic." The term Waldo has of course crept into the everyday slang of scientists and technicians working in the Atomic Energy field. As Isaac Asimov puts it, "A 'Waldo' is a device which when manipulated by the hands transfers the same manipulation to an object at a distance. It is particularly used in handling equipment involving dangerous radioactivity." Do read WALDO if you haven't done so before. — A slightly longer version of H. Beam Piper and John J. McGuire's LONE STAR PLANET (*Fantastic Universe*, March, 1957) is reprinted as A PLANET FOR TEXANS (Ace Double Novels, 35 cents). Warmly recommended. The companion volume is Andre Norton's exciting STAR BORN, also a reprint. — Finally, H. G. Wells' THE ISLAND OF DR. MOREAU (Ace Science Fiction Classic, 35 cents) is described by the publishers, with one eye on a current trend, as "one of the great classics of scientific horror." Be that as it may, the publishers have done well to reprint this novel which first appeared more than sixty years ago.

Cyril M. Kornbluth's A MILE BEYOND THE MOON (Doubleday, $2.95) includes some of the last stories by the author of THE SYNDIC and NOT THIS AUGUST, whose passing, some time back, shocked all of us. Kornbluth would turn a quizzical and slightly cynical eye on the frailties of the individual in that dimly sensed Tomorrow towards which we were—and are—moving, and on the all too likely possibility that we would progress technologically—but not as people. A MILE BEYOND THE MOON is a representative collection of these stories. Recommended.

Theodore Sturgeon is inadequately described by the publishers of A TOUCH OF STRANGE (Doubleday, $2.95) as "one of America's most versatile science fictioneers." There is however nothing pretty-pretty about the world of Theodore Sturgeon, or in his exploration of "the fascinating vagaries of human fears and emotions" (to again quote the publisher's blurb); there is rather a tautness and a tonal perfection, a quality almost of dedication—decidedly rare in the field—which makes the writing of this man so very unique. The present group of stories reflect this quality admirably. Don't miss this book!

George Hunt Williamson and John McCoy's UFOs CONFIDEN-

TIAL (Essene Press, P.O. Box 3433, Corpus Christi, Texas—$3.00) is said to tell "the meaning behind the most closely guarded secret of all time." This may have been the intention, but this column feels the authors (Williamson is a social anthropologist and McCoy a Professor of Parapsychology) fall *rather* short of accomplishing their purpose. Williamson recommends (p. 53) General Count Cherep-Spiridovich's decidedly less than spiritual THE SECRET WORLD GOVERNMENT, a contribution to the hate-literature of another generation, and also suggests (p. 43) that the force behind the "International Bankers" (*i.e.,* the "Hidden Empire") "stems from Communist Russia." He quotes approvingly a statement that top figures in this "secret government" (allegedly responsible for the silencing of some saucer researchers) includes Bernard Baruch, Justice Frankfurter, former Senator Herbert Lehman, and others (p. 43), in apparent ignorance, one hopes, of the implications of such a statement. Mr. McCoy, on the other hand, suggests that the spacecraft appearing today "are under the direction of the hierarchy of their own planets and are working in close harmony with the masters and mystery schools of the hierarchy on Earth." (p. 70) and that the "evolved ancestors" (descendants?) of spatial forces for both good and evil are visiting the Earth at the present time, and that some "space visitors" may represent destructive forces. (p. 89). Mr. McCoy's contribution to the slim volume sharply contradicts the tenor and thinking of Mr. Williamson's early chapters in the book.

Readers may recall our recent warning that some guidance (*not* supervision, mind you) is needed with younger rocket enthusiasts. Now comes an Associated Press story about how an Army missile expert is getting a little nervous about his fan mail. The trouble, says Lt. Col. Charles M. Parkin, is that some of his correspondents "think nothing, apparently, of tucking into their letters enough solid rocket fuel to render me of no service what so ever to anybody." And Lt. Col. Parkin, whose fan mail started after he was called the key man in the Army's program of cooperating with younger rocket enthusiasts, *would* like to be around a while . . .

Asking correspondents to omit fuel samples from their mail, he says, "I expect to slit one of those letters open one day and go immediately into orbit!"

GHOSTS VIVISECTED, by A. M. W. Stirling (Citadel, $3.95), is of interest in view of the distinct possibility that some workers in UFOlogy (saucerdom to you others) may have mistaken psychic phenomena for extra-terrestrial visitations. Mrs. Stirling, who admits to being "allergic to ghosts," and frankly considers it possible that they may be "figments of the same subconscious mind which gives us dreams" (p. 183) writes what the publishers describe as a "brilliant analysis of the manners, habits, mentality, motives and physical construction of ghosts," but which this reader would prefer to describe as a pleasantly rambling and rather loosely knit series of anecdotes, in some instances involving the writer and in others historic personages, anecdotes describing visitations (not from Venus, I hasten to add!), prophetic dreams, and variations on the same. Eminently readable, in a chatty way, the book will give you the feeling (no doubt deliberately so) that you are sitting chatting with Mrs. Stirling about the subject, she, in the meantime, referring to sources on the subject on a nearby shelf, while you disagree, mildly, with her refusal to recognize the implications of some of her own stories.

Science Fiction will, inevitably, often reflect pressures and situations with which we are familiar these days. To this extent, novels such as Louis Charbonneau's extremely effective NO PLACE ON EARTH (Doubleday, $2.95) are perhaps not SF novels in the classic sense, but rather elaborations upon and refinements of a politically amoral pattern of behavior all too familiar to us who remember Hungary in '56.

With this in mind, Charbonneau's novel of a young man imprisoned in a tomblike cell, facing relentless questioning and equally relentless torture, is not only an excellent study of a man's will, crumbling a little under the influence of drugs, but equally so an excellent portrait of a man who has suddenly come to realize the need for combatting this world dictatorship which has rewritten history.

This, I repeat, is not Science Fiction in the conventional sense, but *is* a novel reflecting realities we tend to forget are very much with us. . . . . Recommended.

There were all sorts of reactions to the "Solacon," the 14th World Science Fiction Convention which met in Los Angeles the past Labor Day week end. One correspondent in California reports coming away with "mixed emotions"—she had never attended a science fiction convention before—and a California fan, no doubt thinking of many quiet hours spent drinking orange-juice (we hope) at after-sessions parties, reports that it still seemed "a sort of whirling blur" . . .

This is perhaps understandable, because in between items on the program and the brief but quite lively business session (to judge from tapes we've heard), lots of things happened, including a meeting of the Los Angeles Science Fiction Society at Forrest J. Ackerman's house (where some present are described—not by Forry—as wandering around "in a state approaching ambulatory catatonia"),

a visit to Disneyland (it must have been more than one visit!), and a Grand International Tea Drinking Contest, Robert Bloch and Poul Anderson serving as judges. It seems Djinn Fayne (an interesting name), who represented Catalina Island, completed 23 cups and was declared the winner.

A color film from the "Jet Propulsion Laboratory on the construction and launching of Explorer I" (to quote one report) was shown, also Alan E. Nourse's film, "Born of Man and Woman," and also the first film in a TV series, "Arch Oboler Presents," Mr. Oboler also speaking on Science Fiction in TV. Sam Moskowitz showed 75 slides from his incredible collection of SF cover art. *Fantastic Universe* author Lee Chaytor reports sitting in on a stimulating plotting session with Dr. E. E. Smith and others. And, in between banquet and costume ball (there seem to have been some very interesting costumes, to judge from photos I've seen) and other items on the program, there was a business meeting.

In the last issue we ran Sam Moskowitz's brief article on why he felt that the Annual World Science Fiction Conventions *should* be sponsored by an incorporated body. While there is no disagreement with this basic idea, opinion on the value—or lack of value—of the World Science Fiction Society as a sponsoring society has been rather mixed. Perhaps influenced by recent developments in fandom, it was decided at the business meeting to petition the Board of Directors of the Society to consider a motion for the dissolution of the Society. Since there was some confusion about just who was and who was not a Director—two of the previously elected Directors and the legal officer of the Society resigned during the course of the afternoon—everything appears to have ended on a slightly confused note.

One thing *is* certain, though!

Detroit will be the scene of next years' Convention. *Fine!* I'll be there!

And as for 1960? Why, we'll see you in Washington, of course!

Anchor's TRANSVAAL EPISODE (Essene Press, 48 pages, $1.50) reports on a contact with extra-terrestrials in South Africa. Accent is on Christian Metaphysics. Interesting.

In these days when a young lady named Rona Jaffe seems to be contributing so vividly to the *mythos* about our latterday Kitty Foyles, it may seem rude to suggest that there are other matters of almost equal importance, such as the fact that life is said to have caught up with Science Fiction.

We face a new age these days, a new age that will, within another generation, cause the rewriting of mores and of ways of life rooted in our traditions. Within our lifetimes we have already found ourselves,

to our dismay at times, committed to new responsibilities as a nation and doing things, as individuals or as communities, which contradicted every tradition, every principle, that we had held to be a part of our regional way of life. These pressures, these demands on us to reexamine a number of issues, are of course the by-products of industrial developments long in the making.

But today we are on the treshold of this Space Age—this realization of the dreams of a generation of writers and researchers who realized that, logically, this would come about.

And now?

Must we stand still?

Has Science Fiction nothing more to contribute?

Of course it has!

The field must retain its lead, inspiring the men and the women who will make today's dreams—today's expectations — tomorrow's realities!

This demands imagination—this demands technical know how—*and* it demands a continuing sense of responsibility to today's readers! It demands a resistance to conformism, a resistance to the all too prevalent tendency to translate everything into the simplest comic book terms, a resistance to the demand that life having caught up (as we are told) with Science Fiction, we must now turn back to our ray guns, to our leering monsters, to our horse-operas disguised as inter-galactic adventure novels, to an escapism which does not demand any particular awareness of or interest in whether or not it *is* raining outside on the part of the wide-eyed reader. Suffice it that you are warm. . . .

I believe it has been mildly obvious that I take a dim view of this trend.

We are not living in a vacuum. We cannot disassociate ourselves from the realities of the world around us and take refuge in a pleasantly escapist world of our own, complete with jet-propelled John Carters. This is essential if that Tomorrow we look towards is to have some of that glowing quality we anticipate.

You take a basic proven fact and you extrapolate from there. This, we have often been told, is Science Fiction.

This demands intellectual curiosity.

Not the variant that mutters worn-out socio-economic slogans by rote, ignoring the reality that this is not 1848.

Not the variant that looks for esoteric pie in the sky, that looks for a teacher, any teacher, on whom the chosen may lean, and which misinterprets psychic phenomena as extra-terrestrial visitations and parrots the writings of pseudo-Occultists and Christian Metaphysicians of the last decades with the same monotonous ineptness as the brethren just referred to.

What is needed is intellectual curiosity—and not hardening of the intellectual arteries! What is needed is readiness to speculate—readiness to research (which does *not* mean to consult the nearest Encyclopedia). What is needed is the awareness that we have come this far because in every generation there have been men and women with imagination, men and women with curiosity about the world around them.

Science Fiction *can* and will play a role in this Tomorrow, given the realization of these needs! Do you agree?

There have been a number of interesting reactions to Ivan T. Sanderson's article, MAN-MADE UFO, which appeared in this magazine in the September 1958 issue and was discussed, soon afterwards, on Long John's "Party Line" over WOR. Mr. John McCoy, Professor of Parapsychology and prominent in Contact circles, has written some interesting "Comments Anent Man-Made UFOs," which follow herewith.

The article "Man-made UFOs" by Ivan T. Sanderson in the September issue of *Fantastic Universe*, perhaps is indicative of an important milestone in UFO research and the evolution of thought and opinion in this field. Flying saucer research has long been plagued with mediocre and, in fact, neurotic thought. It has been saddled with the "fringe" elements of groups which are already in their own right, socially rejected. By virtue of this we do find, of course, some brilliant thinkers who are not satisfied to limit themselves to the usual conforming lines of thought. However, we also find at least an equal number of escapists and other individuals afflicted with mental defects ranging from ego-mania to acute paranoia. The resulting chaos is a lamentable mess of conflicting ideas and opinions which generally have little basis in fact. To top it off these ideas are often expounded (or "preached") by individuals who, even if they were working with facts, would be unqualified to hold their self-appointed positions. The above comments do not refer especially to those individuals who have had valid contact with spacecraft from another planet—whoever this may or may not include.

Mr. Sanderson's article regarding Earth-made UFOs or "saucers" depicts a topic about which some of the most illogical thinking in the UFO circles is done. Most dyed-in-the-wool "saucerers" consider it a foregone conclusion that all "saucers" are extraterrestrial. They would not even give a second thought to the possibility that Russia, the United States, or any other country might have been able to construct saucer-shaped aeroforms. This idea is relegated to the realm of the ridiculous (and possibly even the heretical in more "devout" circles).

Nevertheless, there is good evidence from many sources that this is the case—evidently *some* UFOs are Earth-made craft! This concept is quite revolutionary in the ranks of the advocates of extraterrestrial visitation but one of which it must become aware.

There are many vague points in UFOlogy which the "savants" clarify with even more nebulous "explanations." Would Earth-made UFOs offer some solid answers? Perhaps we had better see how this idea would fit into the woof and warp of the UFOlogical tapestry. Suppose that the Russians have developed saucer-shaped craft. Is it possible that they not only are thus responsible for many saucer sightings but also for *some* of the claimed physical "contacts" with "spacemen"? (Indeed, this *is* heresy!) This idea is made more plausible by the fact that in some cases contactees claim that the "spaceman" could speak no English or that it was spoken with a thick accent. What better method to invade a country than to impersonate loving Venusians here to help their brothers of Earth. With the proper propaganda campaign covering many years, they would be welcomed with open arms by almost all. It is likely that the "spacemen" would be requested to take over governmental authority. In fact, it would probably be forced on them. America would be occupied without a shot being fired. If one believes in the internationalist conspiracy which is said to already control the world economically and politically, the concept of Earth-made UFOs takes on even more importance.

Perhaps the above is a little on the fringe of the fantastic, even as are many of the concepts in the saucer field. Nevertheless, since this is mainly directed to the individuals who believe in spaceships, and since Mr. Sanderson's article establishes a firm basis for this type of conjecture, it is felt that this article has fair possibilities of indicating part of the true picture. However, the point to be made in this short commentary is this: shortly, thinking and opinions in regard to UFOs must undergo reorganization and reorientation. Those who always call for open minds must open their own a bit more and examine new evidence even if it is contradictory to their present concepts. The innocently credulous attitude taken by so many, should be replaced with a more critical and objective standpoint. It would, in the light of these comments, be unwise to state a definite belief in the Earth-made UFO unless one had direct knowledge regarding it. Still it *is* obvious that there is surely something to this concept. Thus we must give the topic some attention.

Too many people are attempting to *prove* extraterrestrial flying saucers. This, of course, is not the scientific method. The scientist (whether he has a degree or not) looks at the facts and deduces principles from them. He does not attempt to prove or disprove anything. Personally, the interplanetary UFO has been proven to my satisfaction through my own experiences. However, I do not feel otherworldly visitors would need our puny attempts to evangelize in their behalf. The facts are there for anyone who will look. However, those of us who believe in extraterrestrial visitors and communication with them, will be making a serious error if we continue to disregard factors which may prove to be vital in the future. It is particularly foolish if we ignore them out of prejudice or in an attempt to hold on to an escapism which we desire to believe.

Those who are really interested in penetrating the veil of mystery surrounding the UFOs will do well to be very scientific and critical. Yet they must also be very open to all phases of thought on the subject. Something of great magnitude and of an unknown nature is taking place at present. It has many facets and few if any have any concept of the exact nature of this event. It will take a combination of many present-day ideas and many ideas which are yet to occur to enable us to have the entire story. Thus we must keep the proverbial open mind and carefully scrutinize all facts that come our way. If we do not maintain this attitude, we may as well forget research as we will only "discover" that which placates our own personalities.

man's

castle

by ... Evelyn Goldstein

There were serious problems
that had to be decided at
his coronation — problems a
part of the lives of all . . .

ARNBY had always been master
in his own house. His home was
his castle. His word was its law.
Therefore when they elected him
King of the United Peoples he was
neither amazed nor flustered. He accepted the honor with the calm of
one well suited to the office.

"Do you think I should wear a
crown at the coronation, dear?"
Arnby asked his wife.

Marilee, a small sweet-mannered
woman with soft hair gone gray
answered practically, "Hathaway
did when he was elected king. But
then," she thought a moment,
"Svensky went bareheaded the
time before. I guess it's a matter of
preference. If you'd like a crown
I could make you a splendid one
out of the tiara veil I wore at our
wedding."

He looked fondly at her, "I
think that would be perfect, my
dear. Doubly sentimental."

He gazed about the pleasant
living room of their cottage all
done in bright floral chintz—
drapes on the three long windows,
slip covers on the couch and plump
chairs.

The familiar cherry wood table
was polished fine with a bright

*There has been a lot of speculation about manners and mores in that dimly
seen World of Tomorrow towards which we are moving. Brooklyn writer
Evelyn Goldstein, who will be remembered for* GOD OF THE MIST *(F. U., June
1957) and other stories, makes an attempt to describe that possible Tomorrow.*

brass bowl centered on a wisp of doily Marilee had tatted. He looked out the window to the sunny garden with his hyacinths and roses, and Marilee's stone bordered herb garden. Beyond the full low hedges was Wu Sun's house and after that Washington Smith's. Then the grassy hill went up in a gentle slope and the massive steel structure lorded the crest. That was the castle.

"I shall miss the cottage," Arnby mused, "won't you?"

"Oh, yes. But mostly I shall miss my stone carving. I was getting almost as good at it as Deborah. She's got almost the entire Old Testament etched into Mt. Baldface. But I couldn't work on a mountainside all day as she does. It's so tiring. I find tablets easier, though less sensational. Well, thank goodness I completed Whitman's "Leaves of Grass" . . . in English, Spanish and French."

"For my part I still prefer photography even if it keeps me away from home longer than I like. What were you planning to do next?" Arnby thought Marilee would say Shakespeare or Milton but was not too surprised when she said:

"Houseman. A. E. Houseman. Oh, not all his poems," she added hastily at the look on his face. "But of course, now it's much more important to help you. Affairs of state are so much more arduous." She gave a contented sigh, "I just knew they would recognize your

capacity for organization and administration."

He was pleased at the compliment and asked expansively, "Do you think I ought to pass or repeal any special laws?"

She gave that matter thought. "There's the school . . ."

He gave an angry snort and she amended hastily, "It would be in your jurisdiction . . ."

"Now why should I stop them from vaulting it in? Don't you want it preserved?"

"Oh, I do dear. I do. But there are so few old landmarks left . . . Forget it . . . It was just a—selfish whim . . ." She twisted a sheer handkerchief in her hand, much like a child asking a treat she'd been too naughty to deserve. Arnby knew she was picturing the white frame building in which they themselves had been educated. He knew she thought of the bell with the hempen rope that rang to summon and to dismiss them. He knew she remembered the hard path going out to the east and west roads, trodden to a highway by many children's feet. He had not thought in those days that someday he would be King of it all. Nor had she, in any of her most daring daydreams surmised herself as Queen, residing in the castle that stood on the hill.

"Isn't it strange," she whispered, "how many times I used to wish the school would burn down, or the teachers get sick. And now,

now I would give anything to live those days again . . ."

"Well, that's the way of things. When we're older we regret the youth we wished away. Maybe that's why you chose House-man . . ." He was uncomfortable at the nostalgic turn the conversation was taking. There were just some subjects that were in bad taste. She flushed, guessing his feelings. Hastily she changed the topic.

"What else will you wear at the coronation?"

"I think the dark blue suit. It has a small pin-stripe. That's always very diplomatic, don't you think? And what do you say about a cloak? Could you take that little ermine collar off your old Persian and fix up our royal blue bedspread from upstairs?"

As he had known, her expression cleared. She was a singularly simple person, delighting in a task. He knew her quite well after forty years of marriage. Fondly he said, "I'm so glad, my dear that you are my queen." He leaned toward her confidentially, "You know, twenty years ago I had the great fear that I might be elected King while you were someone else's mate."

Her eyes mirrored sympathetic understanding. "I came close to being Queen when Broderick was King. Fortunately the mating shift had just been voted, and I passed to Kleinwald."

He was still being confidential. "It's too bad the trial matings didn't work out. But I for one am glad they're over and gone. I never wanted another woman but you, my dear." They had always been a reserved couple and did not easily discuss intimate subjects, although much of the reserve had dissolved during the trial matings. He had to admit that, after the initial shock, after the secondary resignation, there had been a certain fascination in the—ah—talents—hidden in the most staid appearing of women. And he supposed she for her side could say the same of men. However in due loyalty and truthfulness he said again gruffly, "It was always you, Marilee."

Shyly she touched his hand, "Nor did I ever love another man."

Reverently he drew her hand through his arm, keeping tight clasp over her small boned fingers. They walked to the windows and looked across the peaceful village to the citadel on the hill.

Tomorrow morning, while the dew was still on the grass, Arnby would stand with Marilee beside him and take his oath:

". . . *do swear as your King to be a wise custodian of the records. To accept into my care, and to catalogue and preserve the lost histories, the lost literatures which you, my subjects, perpetuate on stone insofar as your memories permit. These tablets, and all microfilmed photographs of any sites still remaining, and art treasures or fragments still to be found do I swear* to preserve in the steel and cement vaults in the underground corridors of this, my Castle . . . for as long as the breath remains in me . . ."

And then the new King of the United Peoples would smile down upon his subjects, the hundred odd gray-haired people who had been children when the Atomic War of sixty years before had come and gone leaving sterile Man to fade from the Earth along with other extinct species which had failed the test of existence . . .

too

hot

to

handle

by . . . Norbert F. Gariety

What is the origin of these mysterious rocks? Where do they come from? Are they actually from outer space?

UFO's have intrigued this writer since the summer of 1951. During that year my wife, son, mother-in-law, and dozens of neighbors watched a strange object play "aerial tag," with two Air Force jets over the countryside of upstate New York. Then just as though tired of the game, the *unknown* accelerated into a steep climb and leaving the jets far below, disappeared into space.

Not having been on the spot at the time to view this object, my desire for seeing such an object had to wait until December of 1954. At 7:30 p.m. on December 21st, I personally saw an object, glowing a brilliant white, travel from west to east over Miami. In apparent size, it was ⅓ the size of a full moon, left no exhaust behind it, and traveled from the western horizon to the eastern, in approximately 12 seconds. Five other people reported witnessing the same object, at the same time, the same night.

Unknown to me until the following day, two similar objects were sighted circling over Miami at 2:00 p.m. on the 21st. The sighting was called in to Norman Bean, Director of Engineering Development for a local Miami TV Station.

Norbert F. Gariety is Editor and Publisher of S.P.A.C.E. (Saucer Phenomena and Celestial Enigma), published monthly in Coral Gables, Florida. A former administrative specialist with the Research and Development Command, Air Forces Board, during W. W. II, Gariety served in the Air Force for four years.

Mr. Bean rushed to the roof of the Station building with binoculars in hand, and reached the top in time to see one of the objects and later the second, streak off to the southeast at a terrific rate of speed. A speed which he estimates to have been in the thousands of miles per hour class. The information had been called in to Mr. Bean by employees who had first seen them from Miami International Airport.

Since that day, Unidentified Flying Objects have become a part of my way of life. Collecting data, interviewing eyewitnesses from all walks of life, and public lectures on the topic have become routine. Even when vacationing, UFO's do not take a backseat.

And that is how the *Case of the Mysterious Rocks* came to be investigated. While vacationing in August of 1956, my family and I drove into Erie, Pa., on a Saturday night, to visit relatives. The next morning, an article appeared in the *Erie Dispatch* headlined *"Mysterious Rocks Found Too Hot to Handle."* The news story follows:

"What are they?"
That's what George Traut, of Route 20, Franklyn Ave. Fairview, is asking everyone that views two porous rocks that were found "too hot to handle" for several hours.

Traut reported he spotted the large rock weighing more than 50 pounds, and a smaller one, as he was driving west on 12th, past Cemetery Road, at 12:45 a.m. Saturday.

He stopped his car a few feet away in order to avoid an accident.

When he went to pick them up, Traut said, "They were too hot to handle with bare hands, so I pushed them off the highway onto the berm." A friend "Bud" Buzar was with him at the time.

Saturday morning, shortly after dawn, Traut returned to 12th and Cemetery Road, with a truck and took the unusual rocks to his home.

He said, "They sparkle in the sunlight." But no one knows whether they are pieces of a meteor, plain "Hot Rock" or ——????

I immediately called the Traut residence in Fairview, and made an appointment to go out and look at the mysterious rocks. The Trauts were very cooperative and filled me in on additional details not carried in the newspaper article. I made photographs of the find, and took with me several small pieces of the mysterious substance.

On my way back to Florida, I stopped in Cincinnati, and left a sample with Leonard Stringfield, who at the time was publishing ORBIT a monthly UFO publication. Stringfield turned his sample over to the Chemistry Department of the University of Cincinnati.

Apparently they were not too enthused over the unusual material, as months later Stringfield informed me that the University still had not come up with an analysis. A sample was sent to M. K. Jessup, noted Astronomer and Author, who turned it over to the Smithsonian Institute in Washington, D. C. Just as in the case of the University of Cincinnati, they have never come up with an answer either.

At the University of Miami, the unusual material met with considerably more interest. First to examine the specimen was Dr. Virgil G. Sleight, Geologist at the University. After several days of examination, Dr. Sleight came up with the following conclusions:

(1) *Sample contained no nickel, so it probably was not a meteorite, since known meteorites all contain nickel.*
(2) *Did not look like any rock he had ever seen.*
(3) *Suggested slag — yet was more coarsely crystalline and heavier than most slag.*

Next off the sample of rock went to Dr. Raymond E. Parks, Radiologist at Jackson Memorial Hospital for a Radiation test. His answer was negative.

Next, the sample of mystery rock went to Dr. Russell Williams, well known local astronomer, who after examination made this statement: "Whatever it is, it is not part of a meteorite. And I certainly do not think it could be furnace slag."

About at this stage of the investigation, I received information from Len Stringfield in Cincinnati that a subscriber had sent him a newsclipping of a UFO sighting over Pittsburgh, Pa., on the same date that the Mysterious Rock was found on the road at Erie, 130 miles away.

The Pittsburgh *Sun-Telegraph* ran the following account:

"Mrs. Florence Stauffer reported watching a bright steel-gray ship for more than two hours on Saturday morning. She said, "I don't imagine things. I really saw this thing." Said Mrs. Stauffer, it apparently came from the direction of East Liberty, hovered about for two hours, and then disappeared in a westerly direction. The object was circular and real bright.

In the same wee hours of the morning that a man in Erie finds a most unusual assortment of HOT materials on the highway, a woman in Pittsburgh reports seeing a UFO hover over that city. Pittsburgh and Erie are only minutes away as the UFO flies. Can one be blamed for wondering if the two incidents are related?

The following article which appeared in the *Erie Times* a few days after the rock find is additional evidence of UFO activity in the Erie area.

ITS WINKIN', BLINKIN', AND NAUGHT FOR CIVIL AIR PATROL

Erieites are telling a story about winkin', blinkin', and naught.

Strange lights have been appearing in the sky over Erie.

The Civil Air Patrol has had reports about the mysterious flashes and is now taking steps to identify them.

Observers have been stationed at strategic points in Erie to identify any aircraft or airborne object that might appear.

A Fairview woman told CAP officials that she had been awakened by a "weird" sound. From the window, she saw a light-haloed disk that hovered for a second or two and then sped from view.

A Cumberland Road resident said he spotted a red light 2,000 feet in the air Monday night. It would abruptly change positions and then be still again.

A woman from Lawrence Park reports having seen a series of lights from a single aircraft that moved at an incredible rate of speed.

But the CAP hasn't seen anything. And officials say that most of these things can be explained naturally. They might be cloud reflections, spotlights, tower lights or actual aircraft.

And so we have considerable circumstantial evidence that the mysterious rocks *could have* dropped accidentally or intentionally from a UFO.

The scoffer will immediately say, that the metals dropped off a truck from one of the foundries in the area.

Yet this does not seem to be a reasonable answer. What would a truck be doing carrying hot metals at 1:00 a.m. on a Saturday morning? In addition to this reasoning, as a closeup photograph of the largest chunk of metal shows, one side of the metal is smooth, and shows a gentle curve. It appears to have been formed against a curved surface.

From the amount of curve, it would have been necessary for the metal to have formed against a form at least 10 feet in diameter. Slag pots used in foundries and steel mills are only several feet in diameter. Therefore all logic seems to rule out a foundry as the source of the strange metals.

A sample of the mysterious find was sent to Max Miller, Editor of *Saucers* a quarterly UFO publication in Los Angeles, California. Miller had the sample analyzed by the Smith-Emery Co., Metallurgical and Testing Engineers of Los Angeles. The report of their *Qualitative Spectrographic Examination* follows:

Major Constituent   — Calcium.
Intermediate Constituents — Aluminum, Iron, Magnesium, Manganese and Silicon.
Minor Constituents   — Titanium, Barium, Strontium, Chromium, Vanadium, Zirconium, Boron and Copper.

It is very possible that some of these elements could have been picked up upon contact with the earth, and would not necessarily have been in the original find. But one thing is certain, we do not have just plain ordinary garden variety rocks. In fact they are not rocks at all, but are of a metallic origin and quite a lengthy and impressive list at that.

But the most fascinating evidence in favor of the extra-terrestrial source of the strange metals is yet to come. A sample of the specimen was turned over to Mr. Norman Bean, Director of Engineering Development (as I have said) for a Miami TV Station. Mr. Bean, in addition to being an

active lecturer and researcher on UFO Phenomena is also an expert in his own right on two other equally as interesting and controversial subjects. These are hypnotism and ESP (Extra Sensory Perception).

A close friend of Norman Bean's is a popular Miami hypnotist. For personal reasons requested by this hypnotist, we will not use his name or the proper name of his subject. We shall call his subject Mary Lou.

During a hypnotic session, after Mary Lou had been under for approximately 20 minutes, during which time many and varied questions were asked, the sample of mysterious metal was placed in her hand.

Hypnotist — Can you tell us anything about the material which we have placed in your hand?
Mary Lou — It was a liquid used as a source of power for transportation.

Hypnotist — What do you mean by transportation?
Mary Lou — That means for getting through.
Hypnotist — What do you mean, *getting through?*
Mary Lou — Oh—just flying around.
Hypnotist — Did it come from a Flying Saucer?
Mary Lou — No.—Too much of it was found for it to come from a small ship—
It came from a larger ship—just as an ocean liner carries smaller
boats.
Hypnotist — You mean a *Mother ship?*
Mary Lou — Well—you could call it that.
Hypnotist — What do you mean when you say it was a liquid?
Mary Lou — It was kept in a vacuum sealed container—it is highly dangerous
in the liquid state—but it is not dangerous in its present form.
It escaped, and solidified when it hit the earth's rim.
Hypnotist — What do you mean by the *earth's rim?*
Mary Lou — The earth's atmosphere.
Hypnotist — Was it jettisoned intentionally?
Mary Lou — Oh, No—it is much too valuable for that. It was an accident. It
is a source of powerful energy, much more powerful than any
used on earth.

One week later Mary Lou was hypnotized again, and once more the sample was placed in her hand. When asked what it was she was holding, she said WOOD AND WATER! The sample was wrapped in tissue paper, and Norman Bean quickly realizing that she was reacting to the paper, unwrapped the sample. Once more the answer came out as the week before. "This is a fuel used in transportation." She did not use exactly the same wording as the week before, but gave out with the same identical information.

Later Norman Bean tested the sample on an elderly lady who claims unusual psychic abilities. This woman has in past years made many stage appearances demonstrating her psychic talents. When handed the specimen this lady said that she felt "intense heat."

Subject — There is more than one thing here.
Bean   — You mean more than one element?
Subject — At least half a dozen. I get a sensation of falling. Is this a meteorite?
Bean   — Don't ask me questions. You're doing all right answering mine.
Imagine yourself out in space 100 or 200 miles up. What do you see?
Subject — I see something round—but its not round when you get around the
side of it—it's long.
Bean   — Do you see anything else?
Subject — Yes—I see some small disk shaped objects coming out of the larger
one.
Bean   — How many?
Subject — More than six, but less than twelve. Just like a mother hen and her
chicks.

Norman Bean had not told this lady any previous information obtained on the mysterious metal. Nor did he tell in advance, his next sub-

ject who is a middle-aged Miami man with known psychic abilities. This gentleman was handed the specimen and asked a few questions.

Bean — When you hold this in your hand, what do you get?
Subject — Why—I get a feeling of pain and a sensation of fear in the pit of my stomach. I see the face of a small man—he seems to be both angry and frightened. Why—This doesn't make sense.
Bean — The Hell it doesn't. Suppose you were millions of miles from home and you had just lost part of your fuel. You'd look frightened too!

To add to the unusual evidence already compiled on this mysterious sample of metals, an internationally known Dutch Mentalist, Peter Hurkos, came up with further clues as to its origin.

In the Spring, May of 1957, Peter Hurkos was brought to Miami at the invitation of Henry Belk, 41-year-old scion of a department store fortune. Belk, a graduate of Duke University in 1939, became interested in ESP, while studying under Doctor J. B. Rhine, the famed Duke researcher, who is America's best known authority on parapsychology.

"I believe in this man," Belk told the *Miami Daily News*. "And I haven't a thing to gain out of admitting it. I'm a millionaire many times over. My business is dry goods, but I intend to devote the rest of my life between business and understanding more about this matter of ESP."

Hurkos says, "It all started in 1943 when I fell some 35 feet and suffered a skull fracture. I was unconscious three days and when I came to I had a power beyond that of any man.

"I started telling people I had never seen before some of the most intimate things about their lives. And to my amazement, I found out 85 percent of the time I was right."

The case that gained Hurkos the most attention in Europe involved a firebug, who had confounded Dutch Police by escaping unnoticed after setting dozens of blazes. Brought to the scene, Hurkos immediately led police to a youth who confessed.

"Perhaps I can explain it this way," said Hurkos, "if you see an accident in Miami and see a dead person you carry that with you the rest of your life. If you go away and come back 10 years later you'll still connect the accident scene with death."

Hurkos said that when he gets on the scene of a murder he starts getting mental pictures. "It's just like a film being played before my eyes. I can see things in great detail and I can describe what I see."

Miami has several major unsolved murder cases. One of these is the famous Judy Ann Roberts murder case, unsolved for the past three years. During the Peter Hurkos visit, the *Miami Daily News* ran this item in its columns: "Miami Police, apparently fearing a king size horselaugh from other police departments in the area, haven't officially admitted that Hurkos is going to use what are called his extra sensory perception (ESP) on the Roberts case. But there is no doubt that he is—and at the police's request."

In the several months following Hurkos's Miami visit, the Dade County Prosecuting Attorney, has reopened the investigation in the Roberts case. It is very possible that a break in the case will be forthcoming in the near future.

And here is what Peter Hurkos had to say about the mysterious piece of metal being considered in this article. At a public meeting in the auditorium of the New Age Church of Truth, Miami, Peter Hurkos had his ESP powers tested before more than a hundred spectators. Many items of personal belongings were placed on a central table, by members of the audience.

One after another, Hurkos picked up items and told of personal details of the owners of the items. People that Hurkos had never met and upon whom he had no information. Of one man Hurkos told of an accident the man had had in his youth, and said the man still carried a scar on his right leg. The man verified the information, rolled up his right pants leg, and there was the scar.

The last item Hurkos picked up from the table that evening was the sample of mysterious metal. He showed surprise and said:

"This is a mineral—a combination of minerals.—I do not see it coming from this country—and it does not come from over the water."

Then Hurkos started speaking in a strange language, which seemed to confuse him no end. At first he said, this sounds like Spanish, and then, "But I am familiar with Spanish and Italian, and this isn't either."

"What do you want to know about this metal?"

Norman Bean answered, "Where did it come from?"

Hurkos said, "I see an airship. I see small people—I am sure of it. Very small people. I can see their small hands. I see them living in round houses. Why—they look like FLYING SAUCERS!"

Hurkos then started speaking more of the strange tongue, which was not a gutteral sound, but a very smooth flowing language. "No, this is not Spanish," he said.

During this time Hurkos started to perspire, loosened his tie, and then said, "I have to go now," and left the stage. After the meeting he said, "I have seen these round houses once before."

To some this tale of circumstantial evidence will show that without a doubt this mysterious metal comes from a Space Ship from another World. A ship which accidentally lost a portion of its fuel supply. To others it will be no proof at all. It all depends upon what one will accept as proof.

Capt. Edward J. Ruppelt, three years Chief Investigator for Project Bluebook at Wright Field, says *What Constitutes Proof? Does a UFO have to land at the River Entrance to the Pentagon, near the Joint Chiefs of Staff Offices?*

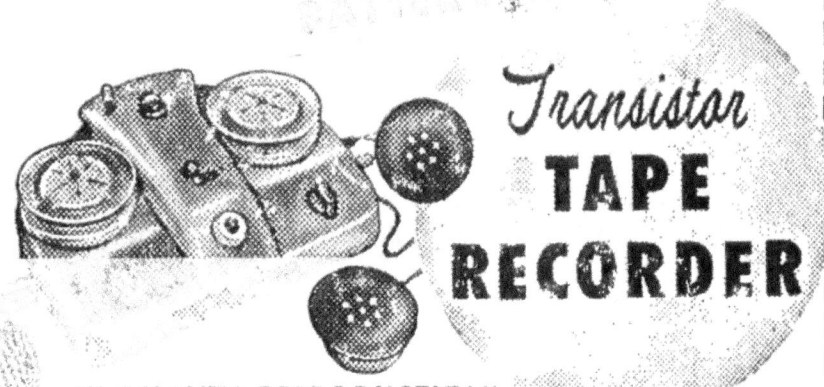